The Bizarre
Adventures
of an
Embezzler

To Bev.

Best Wishes at your
new home.

The Bizarre Adventures of an Embezzler

George F. Ward

To order additional copies of this book, contact:
Xlibris Corporation
1-888-795-4274
www.Xlibris.com
Orders@Xlibris.com
57450

CONTENTS

To my wife and two daughters,
I give my love and thanks for your encouragement.

The Author has enjoyed many years experiencing the outdoors including hunting, fishing, hiking and wildlife photography.

His employment as a Broker in General Insurance has given him insight into white collar crimes and their consequences.

With the advent of D.N.A. and other new methods, the detection of crime has become very sophisticated and anyone involved with white collar crime hoping to avoid detection must indeed be very clever and knowledgeable.

This story of Tim McKay includes his ability to embezzle monies and then escape by using the wilderness in northern Ontario, Canada for his sanctuary.

CHAPTER 1

THE MEETING

After the convocation, Tim McKay met with his favorite professor. After Tim's mandatory word of thanks, the professor said, "I've been thinking about you. Did you know you had the highest I.Q. in your class and, as a matter of fact, the highest of any student in the last ten years. I wanted to tell you, in my opinion, you can probably be a highly successful business-man and make a few million dollars. With more education, I can see you as a great trial lawyer or you could be a clever criminal. We all make choices so I hope your path leads you to a satisfying future.

He was a natural public speaker and also had the ability of an organizer. Eventually, starting his own business was inevitable. He had graduated from Queens University with a Bachelor of Commerce degree (honors) and this had not gone unnoticed by private enterprise who were always looking for the brightest and eventual stars in their chosen fields. The winner out of several was an insurance Company. Advancement was promised and the work was interesting.

His first department was in bonding. He quickly learned how to read financial statements, place mortgages on properties for security, write contract bonds, completion bonds and his employer soon noticed he could separate the chaff from the wheat, avoid the good customers from the bad and his department showed a nice profit at the end of his first year.

To broaden his insurance knowledge, his next appointment was with the crime departments. He learned about burglary, sophisticated locks, theft, hold-up, employee embezzlement and dishonesty, check kiting, book tampering, guns, knives, alarm systems, safe break-in and mysterious disappearance. He took courses offered by alarm companies and he was amazed how many methods were available to catch thieves; from surveillance identification systems to silent alarms to noisy sirens. Companies were inventing new systems on a continuing basis to beat their competitors.

His last appointment was in the liability department. This department was the most interesting of all. Who could sue whom? The usual slip and fall lawsuits were old-hat, mostly sold to retail enterprises. Product liability was tricky. New goods were being invented every day and the manufacturing industry wanted protection for lawsuits. The public in Canada were not as lawsuit minded as their fellow Americans but attitudes were slowly changing. One wanted third party liability protection for blasting a sewer line in a residential area, another for driving a race car, others included drilling wells, demolition of a building in a busy downtown congested street, installing a church tower, manufacturing parts for a gun, outdoor rock concerts and golf tournaments. It was tricky trying to figure the lawsuit exposure to the public and then getting an adequate premium. He studied differences between trespassers, invitees and licenses. He learned about hold-harmless agreements, negligence, world-wide endorsements and how to exclude exclusions. The policies contained care, control and custody clauses and he felt like he had completed a minor law degree when he had finally finished studying liability insurance. Court cases kept changing the rules and it behooved the insurance underwriter to keep aware of legal proceedings with new rulings and judgments. He loved reading about Court cases, the arguments given by the lawyers and the decisions handed down by Judges.

But the day came when he tired of working for someone else, adhering to their rules, waiting for the benevolent pay increases, promotions, and he did not suffer well his fellow workers that were not as brilliant as he. He turned his mind and time investigating money-making companies and exploring new ideas.

Finally, he settled on a new venture; one that could make him a lot of money, cause a bankruptcy or send him packing back to an employer. He would be self-employed.

His letter was sent to hundreds of C.E.O.'s and President's of Companies that he found in a Who's Who Business Directory and some from the telephone yellow pages. He knew that when you have a business, the old adage held true, "If you want your business to shine, then don't hide your light under a basket . . . . advertise."

His letter read:

> To all Executive Officers,
> Presidents,
> Managers.
>
> How many ways can your Company have a loss, sometimes crippling and sometimes devastating?
> This seminar is to familiarize you with insurance coverages and protective methods. A panel of experts will speak on many types of property insurance, crime insurance, lawsuit exposures and preventive methods.
> NO ONE IS SELLING YOU INSURANCE OR EQUIPMENT!
> The fee is $250 for a full day of information and attendance is limited to 200 Executives. A light lunch will be served and there will

be a question and answer period after 4 p.m. Private consultations can be arranged at a future date at a fee of $500 per hour.

This is a rare opportunity to examine the future of your business. Don't take a loss because of lack of knowledge! Call 1-800-_____

Signed,

Tim McKay, B.Comm. (honors)

The quiet millionaire sat in the back row of the filled hall and was slightly bored. He had a good insurance broker who placed insurance for him on his radio station, newspaper and property development business. He had listened to his broker explain coverages, deductibles, exclusions and premiums but he figured it was worth $250 to hear about all sorts of coverages from another expert. Having a skeptical nature, he always wondered if there were coverages he should have or coverages that could be self-insured. Victor Tobiah wondered if he went to Asia and got kidnapped, how much ransom money would his captors want. How much would kidnapping insurance cost? He did not carry errors and omissions insurance for mistakes in his newspaper and radio business and thought maybe he should inquire about the premium

The seminar opened with a pretty girl introducing Tim McKay and he appeared on stage with an air of confidence. He told his audience, since it was only a one day lecture, insurance coverages, alarm systems, lawsuit protection and other matters could only be highlighted but he would give them a check-off sheet to take home with them and they could review it with their own insurance broker. He again told them to relax about any high-pressure salesmanship because as he had mentioned in his letter, he was not selling or promoting any insurance Brokers, Insurance Companies and that included alarm and identification vendors

Victor Tobiah became mesmerized with the discussions on fraud, embezzlement, employee dishonesty and other stealing methods where he might lose a lot of money. He had made a few million dollars, maybe close to a billion and he was not prepared to let anyone take it from him in an illegitimate way and he knew a clever person possibly could swindle him. Tim McKay seemed to know a lot about cheating, stealing, embezzlement and the many ways one person could beat or flimflam another. At the close of the meeting and after the usual mundane question period, Victor Tobiah intercepted Tim McKay as he was leaving the meeting and asked him if he would see him at his office, about two hundred miles away. He said he would pay McKay the fee of five hundred dollars an hour for his time plus traveling expenses. His business card read

> VICTOR TOBIAH
> Kingston, Ont.
> North End Shopping Plaza,
> Unit 1.
> (unlisted telephone number)

A time was suggested for January 30th, at 11 a.m., over two months away and Tim McKay agreed to the time and place. They discussed the fee of five hundred dollars and $150 for traveling expenses. Victor Tobiah agreed.

McKay arrived on the arranged date about two hours early. He toured the waterfront, watched the ferry carrying cars, examined the business section, admired the old limestone buildings and finally it was time to meet Victor Tobiah. They left the office and went to an exclusive men's club. A steward took their drink orders, Tobiah a scotch malt and McKay a soft drink.

"I have an unusual proposition for you," Tobiah started. "If at any time you don't want to hear any more of my offer, tell me to stop. You must agree now that the conversation is being done in absolute secrecy and I must have your verbal assurance of future silence."

Trying not to look surprised, McKay replied, "you mean this meeting has nothing to do with your insurance, alarm systems or anything that was in my address?" Tobiah said, "that's right so let me start with my proposition." He ordered another scotch and looked at McKay directly. "I don't suppose you have ever heard of the E.O.G.S." McKay shook his head in the negative and Tobiah said, "I didn't think so because there are only twenty people in the world that are aware of this organization or club. I again remind you that this is never to be mentioned by you to anyone, ever."

"McKay was getting a little impatient, frowned and said," I told you I agreed to this conversation with my guaranteed confidentially, so go ahead, my time is costing you money."

Victor Tobiah made sure they were seated in a secluded place in the plush men's club, lowered his voice and said, "EOGS stands for Eastern Ontario Gambler's Syndicate. The Members are all millionaires or billionaires and we gamble on various things. We do not bet on horse or dog races. We may bet on the outcome of an election, the value of the Canadian dollar on a certain date, the decisions made by the Supreme Court in Canada or in the United States and maybe the value of certain stocks in the market-place at a future date. We have very few limitations and some of the bets are very unusual and imaginative.

"These bets are large, sometimes amounting to a million dollars or more and this syndicate may subscribe to a bet individually or within the twenty as a group. There has never been anything in writing and there has never been any one person or syndicate that refused or have been unable to pay their losses."

McKay interjected, "O.k., so you guys are big, big shooters, where do I come into the picture?"

"We recently had a discussion and some of us calculated that someone, a clever person could embezzle or cheat many financial places and not get caught. Others say the person would get caught, maybe immediately or soon after the cheating was discovered."

Tim McKay stared at Victor Tobiah and said, "Are you implying that the person with that lying, cheating and embezzlement ability might be me?"

Tobiah answered, "Yes, but hear my proposition. Some of us want to bet that a person could steal or embezzle one million dollars from several financial places and not get caught. Here is my offer. You obtain a total of one million dollars from ten or more financial places and not get caught. We would pay you five hundred thousand dollars if you can do this and not be convicted within a twelve month time period after you have received monies from your last illegal transaction In addition, we would pay you up to two hundred thousand for your expenses within the twelve month period."

McKay sat silent for a few moments. "Of course, I would have to mull this offer over but I have a couple of questions. How could you know if I, in fact, obtained this amount of money?" He added, "And how would I send you my expense account since I am not prepared to give you anything in writing?"

Tobiah promptly said, "Our betting syndicate has many of our members in high places in the community and we could quickly find out if the cheated financial places had suffered a loss and moreover, we can determine and find the amount swindled from each place. After you advised me you had finished with the last target place, we would start our investigation to certify your numbers. As far as the expense account is concerned with a maximum of two hundred thousand, I would give you a private unlisted telephone number and you can say, as briefly as possible, the amount of the expense and the reason. We will not argue with you. We will deposit the money in a special account, known only to you and myself. Any more questions?"

McKay said, "Oh, yes, there are several, providing I am interested. Let's meet two months from now and we will finalize the terms but likely I will refuse to enter into such a bizarre idea. If I got caught with this white collar crime, it could mean between five, ten or even twenty years in prison plus a very hefty fine. I am now leaving our meeting and, I promise you, no one will ever know of this conversation unless you try and cheat me if we proceed."

Now, give me my payment of one thousand dollars for two hours of my time plus my travel expenses of two hundred dollars."

Tobiah reached in his pocket, unfolded a large roll of money and gave McKay twelve hundred dollars.

McKay stood up to leave and said, "I don't suppose you want to tell me the amount of money you can win on this bet if this scheme is carried out successfully?"

With a smile, Tobiah said, "I will tell you this. You would be amazed at the size of the bet and no, you will never know the amount." He added, "Here is a private telephone number you can call me anytime and leave a message but don't give any details, be as brief as you can. The phone will be set-up to accept incoming calls from you only. And, I might add, I will be the only person in our syndicate that will know your name and address."

On the two hour drive home, Tim McKay could not believe such a bizarre idea had been offered to him. With his quick mind, he formulated what needed to be done to commit the crime and escape punishment. By the time he reached his Toronto office, he was excited but, Victor Tobiah would not know of his decision for a couple of months. McKay had good reasons for delaying his acceptance to Tobiah.

CHAPTER 2

THE DISGUISE

It took a month. The office lease was cancelled and a two month penalty was paid. The apartment was closed and the key given to an elderly female neighbor who agreed to dust and vacuum for one hundred dollars a month. The telephone service was terminated, the hydro agreed to an automatic monthly withdrawal payment plan and he gave his landlord two dozen postdated cheques for two thousand dollars each. His female assistant was given her termination notice and all future attendees at his lectures were given refunds with a regret-letter for the cancellation.

McKay knew that someday the police might inquire if anyone knew of a person making a sudden disappearance. He would circulate a story about a tourist going abroad for an extended holiday.

Relatives, friends and business associates all were asking similar questions.

"When will you be back?"

"In about two years, but no definite timetable."

"Where can we reach you if an emergency occurs?"

"You can't"

"Maybe it is a little insensitive to ask, but are you taking a girlfriend with you?"

"No, this is a solo trip but, it doesn't mean I might not meet some cutie overseas."

"How are you traveling? Are you renting a car, going by train or bus?"

"I haven't decided yet. Maybe all of them."

"Where are you going? Mostly to Europe? Are you going to Asia or Africa?"

"This a two year rambling holiday but I hope to see a lot of sights I have read about and, as you know, I really enjoy history so I plan on visiting a lot of historical places."

And then, he tolerated with feigned interest the usual suggestions.

"If you are in the south of Spain, make sure you visit Rhonda, Mijas and the Alhambra."

Another said, "You must visit Ireland. We visited the south part, saw the Cliffs of Moher and even kissed the blarney stone. Try that Guinness Beer, although we found it a little strong compared to Canadian beer.

An old friend had just returned from France and said, "If you are in Paris, visit the Moulin Rouge. It was a little pricey with the dinner show but, what the hell, a person only lives once. I know you like history so make the Louvre a must while in Paris. There is always a damned line-up to see that painting of Mona Lisa and personally, I didn't think the painting was all that great."

Everybody had advice.

"I don't know when you will be in Scotland but once a year, they have one of the world's biggest tattoos, that is, if you like the bagpipes. And Edinburgh Castle is magnificent. I don't know if you play golf or not, but try to see the Old Saint Andrew Golf Course.

McKay was patient as possible and he was told about spas in Germany, boat trips on the Rhine River, the Alps in Switzerland and on and on and on.

His two year trip overseas was believed and everyone wished him a happy holiday. He was satisfied he had planted a good cover story.

He needed two new passports, driver's licenses and medical cards. He was now both Harry Bennett and Larry Johnson. The forgery was expensive at five thousand dollars a set but he would recover this money from Victor Tobiah.

He crossed the border in February at the Ivy Lee bridge. The American Custom Officers asked him to come inside their little Custom's office and inquired why he was entering the United States and where was he going. He explained he was going to Hutchinson Island, a barrier island off the coast of Florida and he was hoping to find a winter retreat for his wife and children. It was to be their surprise. The Custom Officers viewed his license plates on their computer but the rental card gave them no information. The criminal record for Harry Bennett was also examined but it gave a clean-bill-of-health. The real Harry Bennett lived quietly in Toronto and had never had even a speeding ticket. They inquired when they might expect his return and he calculated two weeks. The Officers wished him a safe and pleasant trip, satisfied they had not permitted a terrorist to invade their country.

He traveled southbound. It occurred to him the Americans might keep track of his progress so he occasionally turned off the highway, into a small town and then back to the main highway. He was sure no one was following him. Eventually, he headed south-west towards Texas. It was two days of hard driving before reaching Austin where he checked into a cheap motel. He paid cash and the attendant did not ask for identification. He slept that night and most of the next day.

The live theatre was advertised in the yellow pages and with a bribe of ten dollars the caretaker permitted him to enter by a side door which said, "NO ENTRANCE except for staff and entertainers." Tim wandered past several closed doors until he found one ajar, peeked in and said hello to a woman wearing a paint covered smock whom he guessed to be around thirty years of age.

She saw him, frowned and said, "What the hell are you doing in here? This place is not open for the public." She started to close the door but he held it open and said, "Hi, I'm Harry Bennett from Corpus Christie and I wanted to talk to someone in the make-up department."

"Listen, there all sorts of weirdos, creeps and stage-door Johnnys hanging around theatres, now scram before I call the police."

He gave her his best smile and replied, "Just wait a moment. I'm here to offer a make-up artist a business deal. I have no interest in your actual theatre. Are you in charge of the department?"

"Yes, I'm in charge of costumes, make-up and disguises. Now, okay, tell me what you want."

Tim backed up not to alarm her and said, "This isn't the place to discuss my proposition. Could we meet for coffee at a public place later today."

This seemingly harmless request appeared to have calmed her and she replied, "Well, if it is strictly business with no funny stuff like sex or something strange, I'll meet you in two hours at the coffee shop next door. It is called the Coffee Shop and Grill. Now, get the hell out of here, I'm trying to get ready for the next show."

Tim said, "Great, I'll be there." At the little restaurant, she joined him at a back table and without smiling, she said, "I'm Ethel Grant. You said your name was Harry Bennett?" He smiled and replied, "I'm applying for my first acting job at Corpus Christie and I have no experience. I lied to them but now I need some help to get the job and I'm willing to pay for your time and expertise. Do you have an hourly rate? I was hoping maybe I could pay you three hundred dollars for a full day. I want to look like a middle-aged man, maybe around fifty years of age, a little taller, heavier and perhaps with a mustache. I guess some gray in the temple part of my hair would be good, too. I also would like to have a slight tan."

Ethel Grant smiled for the first time. "I can do that but there would be two conditions. Firstly, I don't know you so I would like to have a chaperon with me. Secondly, I would want my money in advance, in cash, and fifty dollars for the chaperon although she isn't doing anything but watching. Tomorrow, the theatre is blackened so we could do the work in my make-up room."

"Wonderful. Here is three hundred and fifty dollars and I'll see you at nine tomorrow morning."

She was an expert.

Ethel said, "Get a piece of paper and write down some of the things I'm going to tell you about changing your looks. You obviously need to buy some things. I can sell you some of the items but other make-up materials can only be bought by mail-order. There are only a few stores in the States that sell make-up materials and I can order them for you if you want."

"Let's start with the hair. You must buy an expensive wig. They are the types made in Eastern Asia. The hair is stripped of the cuticles, bleached and then dyed. You know, I can spot a cheap rug on ladies and men's hair so don't be a cheapo with your money when buying a wig.

"You want a slight tan. Today I'm using a triangle applicator sponge but you should buy a natural sea sponge. They wash easier for re-use."

"If you are wearing a suit coat, you will need an undergarment to give you a heavier weight. There are various types and sizes. How much heavier do you want to be?"

He thought for a moment and replied, "I weigh one hundred and sixty pounds and my new look should be a man weighing about two hundred. This new man probably has a paunch from the good life with drinks and food."

Ethel Grant looked him over and said, "We could probably add two inches to your height with elevator shoes and making you heavier is easy.

I want to tell you a secret about your disguise. You must think like an older man, talk a little slower but not stupidly and bend over a little because of your arthritis. Sometimes wear a fedora because you think they are still in style. If you are asked a question, ponder it a little, don't be flippant or a wise guy.

Will you be a rich man, middle class or poor?" He thought for a moment. "I will be quite rich."

She said "then think and talk like someone who is loaded. Did you ever notice that most rich people have an air of confidence? The disguise is just part of your trickery. Acting is the key. Don't be nervous. For example, if you were walking with someone on a street and a really beautiful expensive car drove past, just glance at it as if you were not greatly impressed. Have an air of authority. That intimidates people."

Almost a full day had passed and they both were tired. Tim said, "You have been great today. Could I take you to a nice restaurant for dinner?" Ethel looked at him and replied, "Okay, but no nonsense. Dinner, one glass of wine and I'll get a taxi home. I'll pick the restaurant and meet you there. Is that agreeable with you?"

After dinner and three glasses of wine, she said, "I can do you a favor. I'll order all your make-up material and have it delivered to the theatre. Can you give me two days and I'll have it here by delivery express."

"Wonderful. I would really appreciate that. I'll need enough for about one year."

As they were finishing their coffee, Ethel said, "I don't believe you are from Corpus Christie and, as a matter of fact, I don't believe you are from Texas either. Are you planning on robbing a bank or something illegal? You have a northern accent."

Tim smiled, "Ethel, you are clever but, I can't tell you right now why I need the disguise. I am not from Texas but if you will give me your telephone number, some day I'll tell you all about it. You will find it to be an intriguing story."

Two days later he left for Canada. He wanted no record anywhere of his trip or buying a disguise so he shaved and washed in truck stops and slept in his car when he got tired. There would be no paper trail of his trip. The Canadian Custom Officers asked him about purchases and he re-iterated his story about Florida. He told them he had bought his children some fun play-time make up materials. They didn't search his car, wished Mr. Bennett a safe trip and Tim headed for home thinking about the next step of his embezzlement plan.

From his years in the insurance business he knew some private investigators and the best was Peter George. They met in a motel room and McKay said, "I want some information on six bank managers and three Credit Union managers.

Peter George had had lots of requests over many years and he stared at McKay and said, "Look, if you are going to rob these financial places, I don't want to be involved."

McKay replied, "No, there will be no robbery. I am doing a secret research investigation for a Government Agency. This meeting and your report must never be known to anyone. I have made a list of the information I want.

Their names, home address, married status, the number of children and ages, service club associations, hobbies like golfing, curling or bridge. I want to know about previous marriages and their history such as place of birth and any other occupations before they entered the banking field. Generally, when I meet them I want to talk to them like I am an old friend so I need to know everything about them."

"Can you do this job without any paper trail?"

Peter George thought for a moment and said, "Yes, but you must pay me in cash and my fee is one hundred dollars an hour plus expenses, in cash. I will give you a report and that will be the only piece of paper in existence. Obviously, I won't be paying income tax on the money you pay me so I guess we will have to trust each other regarding secrecy."

"There is just one thing. If you are doing anything illegal, don't tell me about it."

McKay said, "I've known you for a long time since my years in the insurance business, and I promise you, absolutely no one will ever know that you prepared this report. When you send me this information, don't put it on any letterhead and don't sign it. Just a plain piece of paper so there will be no trace to you. I'll pay you in cash"

"When can we meet again?"

The private detective said, "Actually, this investigation is routine for me. I should be finished in three weeks."

After finding a one bedroom apartment, Tim bought a full length mirror. He was going to transform into a different person with a new name, Larry Johnson and for a week, Tim practiced wearing his new make-up, changing his walk, speaking a little slower with a slight Scottish accent and carrying a cane for a slight limp. There must not be any evidence and in the apartment he wore surgical gloves and outside his apartment he would coat his fingers with an un-noticeable clear solution which left no prints. He practiced writing with his left hand. The small apartment was leased for one year. The furniture was rented and the rental car was big and impressive. A little office was located at the rear of a shopping plaza; the rental desk, filing cabinet, two chairs and a computer including an internet filled the small space. New clothing was purchased for his larger body, two pairs of elevator shoes, a cane which he would use from time to time and a fedora. His appearance, attitude, talk and deportment needed to be impressive. For his cover story he wrote a commercial newspaper advertisement saying

EMPLOYERS

DO YOU NEED AN EXPERT EMPOYEE?

A new concept to help you find the right experienced person for your business with Competitive rates.

LARRY JOHNSON EMPLOYER SERVICE

He had no intention of taking on any clients but if necessary, to protect his identity, he would go through a charade.

He needed a resume and a financial statement, something that would impress the bankers but without too much fluff. He was ready for his first victim, but now, his required phone call to Victor Tobiah was needed.

"Tobiah, ready to proceed as per our agreement. Partial expense account to follow" McKay. He had no intention of telling Tobiah about any or all of his preliminary planning.

CHAPTER 3

THE TARGETS

While he waited for information from private investigator Peter George, he practiced applying facial coloring, wore his non-magnifying glasses, had an ophthalmologist change his gray-green eyes to a deep brown with contact lenses, walked with elevator shoes, spoke with a slight Scottish brogue, tried his fedora at different angles and adjusted the girdle for his enlarged girth size. He had decided to wear a mustache and experimented with size and placement for a man his new age. He wrote long sentences with his left hand signing his new name thousands of times. He was finally satisfied his signature appeared very natural.

The investigation from Peter George was done and he and Peter discussed the results about Bankers while they drank coffee in his car.

"Everybody seems normal. I mean, there are no dark hidden secrets from any of them. No girlfriends, excessive alcohol, drug use, excessive betting or criminal activities. Some of them have speeding tickets but they have all been modest. There are some small bets made at the golf course but it involves under ten dollars each game."

The fee of two thousand dollars was paid to the Investigator and the next few days he studied the reports for each bank and the credit union managers. He was ready for his first target. He needed to become their friend as quickly as possible

The receptionist bade him a good morning and said the Manager Mr. MacLeod would see him in a few moments. He was ushered into a modest office, said "good morning, my name is Larry Johnson and added, "I'm a new person to your city and since I wanted to open a new account with your bank. I thought I should meet the head man." Manager MacLeod said, "thank you, welcome. Let me get the person who opens new accounts and she will be happy to look after you. What brings you to our City?" He had rehearsed his story many times. He settled in the visitors chair and replied, "I was a financial advisor and stock broker in Montreal and after my wife died, I wanted to go to smaller city to escape the heavy traffic, smog and the fast pace. I did very well financially with several investments but now I'm changing my career. I guess you could call it almost semi-retirement. I'm opening a business which will find executive employees for large and prosperous companies. My fees are a little outrageous but if big companies want top-notch employees they are willing to pay the price to get them." Manager Harold replied, 'that's very interesting and if we can offer any of our bank services, let me know. I'm tied up right now with appointments and phone calls but give me a call soon and we can spend some more time together".

The next bank treated him much the same and the third bank manager welcomed him and introduced him to the department supervisors including the loan officer.

At the fourth bank, the manager welcomed him and told him the loan department was open to help him if he needed assistance. He called on the fifth bank and then three Credit Unions. At each place, he deposited ten thousand dollars and told each there would be more deposits in the near future. He had deposited $80,000 of his own money and eight doors had opened. The following week he deposited $5,000 at each place and asked to see the loan officer. He told each of them that he had had a line of credit with his previous bank in Montreal and he would like to establish an amount at their bank. On inquiry, he lied and said, "My previous line of credit was one hundred thousand dollars but I would be happy with seventy thousand". They were cautious and said they would let him know. He replied, "Would you like a financial statement?" This un-solicited offer pleased them and he said he would have one within a few days.

He applied to all the credit card companies and they quite willingly gave him a purchase limit of $10,000 plus a loan limit of $5,000 at an interest rate of 23% annual when he borrowed their money.

At each bank, he naively asked the difference between demand loans, lines of credit, mortgages overdrafts and the rate of interest for each. He tried to appear interested as each person gave him a lesson on borrowing money. Larry Johnson mentioned to each that he might be buying a winter home in Florida but at this time, he did not need any help with bridge financing.

The various Bank Managers wanted to gain his commercial account and to please them he resultantly joined the Kiwanis Club, The Sales and Advertising Club and the Yacht Club. He had bought a McGill University ring and flashed it for impression wherever he went and it didn't go un-noticed

He completed an un-audited financial statement and gave a copy to each Loan Officer. The un-solicited gesture on his part impressed the Managers and it added to his growing creditability. Since he was not borrowing any money, no one bothered to confirm the statement.

Single family home in Montreal presently rented	$325,000.
(mortgage of $68,000 remaining at 6% interest)	
Twelve Plex apartment building	$980,000.
(Fully rented with mortgage of $380,000 at 7%)	
Cash in hand	$61,000.
Canadian Government guaranteed certificates	$100,00.
(due in two years paying 3.4% annual compounded)	

stock in a dividend mutual fund (banks)	$51,000
Registered Retirement Savings Plan	$180,000
(payable at age 65)	
Bank Loan—Canadian Bank of Commerce	$31,000
Automobile—snowmobile—household contents	
and miscellaneous assets	$80,000

He showed his debts with current accounts payable such as telephone, hydro, a small credit card balance, car repairs, rent, clothing and other small items. There was nothing overdue past sixty days. The total was $839.

Each financial place filed away this statement and thanked him. He omitted to show details normally required within a financial statement but the financial places did not investigate or confirm details because they had not been asked to loan Larry Johnson any money.

He had learned of a new mortgage fraud. A counterfeit deed was obtained on several homes. The homes were of middle-class value and they all had small first mortgages remaining or no mortgage. When the time was ripe, he would apply for a second mortgage in the amount of $50,000 each from independent second mortgage lenders. He chose six homes for this embezzlement. The innocent homeowner would not be aware of this new lien transaction until the first payment was required.

He flew to Florida under the name of Larry Johnson and had letterhead and envelopes printed which said,

Sidney C. Swartz,

Attorney at Law,

Federal Building,

St. Augustine, Florida

U.S.A.

82333

The letter said—

Mr. Larry Johnson has purchased a home at 1072 Sea Drive in St. Augustine in the amount of $220,000 through the Ocean and Sand Realty Company. The vendor is William Anguilla of Rochester, New York.

In order to close this sale, we require a down-payment of 25% or $55,000. Will you please send a money transfer in this amount, payable, In Trust, to myself? It is important that this money be received within two days prior of the closing date as noted on the attached "Offer To Purchase" or this realty purchase transaction will not close as other offers have also been received by Mr. Aguilla.

The letter was signed—Sidney Swartz, Attorney At Law.

McKay hired a Florida overload personal employment office and told them to mail this letter on a certain date when ordered; they were also to collect and forward any mail to him at his Canadian address and send it by priority mail. He gave them a key to the newly acquired post-office box in St. Augustine and he opened a bank account in St. Augustine depositing $500 dollars.

Tim McKay courted the good-will of the various Managers and Loan Officers and he visited their respective places as often as possible on various pretexts by ordering blank checks, picking up their sales literature, getting change, making deposits, withdrawals and inquiring about current interest rates. The information from Peter George was invaluable. With two of the Managers he discussed hockey. There were draft choices, trades, scores, suspensions and opinions on coaching in the local Junior A league. With another Manager, he talked about baseball; who was leading the league with runs batted in, pitching statistics, world series favorites and franchise changes. The golfing world always had something that was news; the bridge hands that were printed in the paper each night were always good for a discussion and he felt that listening to *their* travel stories was met with favor. He had learned to be a good listener and he sometimes sprinkled the conversation with some philosophy or humor.

He realized the longer he masqueraded as Larry Johnson, the more dangerous a discovery might become and the embezzlement would fail. Jail, embarrassment, loss of reputation and a Court Ordered Community Service would happen if he failed. He set himself a date for the fourth week in April.

In the second week of April, McKay told each Bank Manager he had decided to buy a summer home in St. Augustine. He told them he would use his line of credit for a down payment and they would receive a letter from his Florida lawyer.

Falsified deeds had been printed and second mortgages were arranged on six homes for $50,000. He borrowed $5,000 each from four credit card companies and he asked the five banks to deposit his pre-arranged line of credit to his account. He was to embezzle one million and he now had exceeded that amount by ninety-five dollars.

His expenses had been more than he had anticipated and he jotted a very brief note to Victor Tobiah.

I will collect my expenses for the amount listed below by cash at your office for the following. Tobiah had agreed to an amount up to $200,000.

2 passports	10,000
Advice on make-up	350
Traveling	700
Make-up material	2,000
Motel rooms	200
Investigations	2,000
Apt. rental	12,000
Rental car	3,000

Computer	900
Apt. contents rental	4,500
Secretary	250
Outdoor purchases	3,700
Meals	1,800
Entertainment	560
Vehicle purchase	4,000

ISSUE CHEQUE FOR $43,960. IMMEDIATELY

A week later, he purchased a used 6 year old van for $4,000.

The embezzlements were completed.

It was time to disappear. All the money had been received including the maximum loans from the Credit Unions and the Credit Card Companies. He notified Tobiah of the places that had been swindled for his verification. After receiving the Lawyer's letter, each bank had sent Lawyer Swartz fifty-five thousand dollars for the bridge financing. McKay flew to Florida, collected the checks, converted them to cash, closed the bank account, the post office box, paid the Secretarial Overload their fee and returned home. After his demand to Tobiah, he had called his office and collected forty-three thousand, nine hundred and sixty dollars, paid in cash.

The apartment was washed and then sterilized with a strong commercial cleanser. He had worn surgical gloves when in his apartment and car and, just in case, the rental car was also sterilized for fingerprint evidence. He notified his landlord he was taking a month's holiday and the rental place was told they could pick up the household contents a month later. He left the City after closing all his bank accounts.

Including the swindled money and the recovery of his own original money, he had a million, six hundred thousand in his possession. All the Larry Johnson clothes and disguises were burned at a picnic camp site and he became Tim McKay again. As he traveled north, he started to purchase camping equipment. Each city had an outdoor store and he bought some supplies at each place. He did not want anyone's awareness someone had purchased a huge supply of equipment and slowly, from city after city, his van filled. In the City of North Bay, he rented a safety deposit box and placed in it one million, five hundred thousand. He drove for two days until he reached the Town of Hearst where he found an airport which had several float planes in the adjoining lake.

CHAPTER 4

THE SANCTUARY

The fellow was pushing papers around the desk when Tim McKay arrived. The airline shack contained the usual office equipment plus a radio system that Tim concluded were the required systems for transmissions to aircraft. Photographs were on the walls showing float planes landing and throwing spray from the pontoons. There were also pictures of lakes and islands and a picture of the little white air base building.

"Are you one of the pilots," Tim asked and the man replied, "yup, one of the best, that's how I got the nickname Ace. Did you want to go on a little flip? Pretty country out there if you haven't seen it before. Got room for three passengers. Is anyone else with you?" Tim nodded in the negative and said, "I've got an unusual proposition for you." Ace said, "Go ahead, I'm listening." Tim continued, "This is just between you and me. There is something very unusual I want to ask you." Ace stared at him for a moment. "I can keep my mouth shut when I have to so go ahead."

Tim pulled out a map and showed him a little lake about one hundred miles north. "I want to go camping here for a long time. I want to go to-day and be picked up early October or before freeze-up. That could be between five and six months. Firstly, can we fly in to-day? Ace looked at the wall clock

THE BIZARRE ADVENTURES OF AN EMBEZZLER

and said, "Sure, if we leave pretty soon. I suppose you have a lot of food and gear to pack if you're going for that long. I can tie the canoe on one of the pontoons so that's no bother. Do you want to know the cost?

It will be five hundred dollars. Does that suit you?"

Tim nodded yes at the price but continued, "There is more to the trip than just flying in and out. It has to be confidential. As a matter of fact, you can't enter the trip in your log book It must be secret."

"Good God man, I can't fly anyone anywhere without logging the trip. It would cost me my license. Do you realize that I would be the only person to know where you are camping? If I got sick or died, no one would come and get you if it isn't logged. And my friend, there is no way you are going to walk from that lake to civilization. It is full of lakes, swamps, muskeg, creeks and heavy bush. You couldn't do it. After freeze-up, you would die unless you were an Indian or trapper who can live in the bush during winter. Why don't you want anyone to know where you are?"

"I've been asked to do a secret research project for the Government and that's all I can tell you. I realize what I'm asking is illegal for you. Would you take an extra one thousand dollars to fly me in, pick me up with no record of the trip?"

"I have a suggestion", Tim added, "you could log the trip and then say I changed my mind about the destination while flying. Just log you took me to a different place? My trip must be confidential or I can't go."

Both men sipped their coffee in silence. Finally, Ace said, "okay, I'll do it but let me make a suggestion. Every two weeks I'll do a fly-by past your camp-site. You might need me. For example, if you are sick, no food or just have to return. I'll pick you up. The signal is a long stick stuck in the lake just out from the beach with a white clothe attached. I fly supplies to different places for mines, logging companies and trappers so it wouldn't be much out of my way to veer off to your camp-site and check on you. The log book would show you at a different place. Geez, you really want to be isolated, don't you?"

"Okay, that's a deal. I'll give you one thousand dollars now and the other five hundred when you pick me up."

"Nope, sorry, I want the full payment to-day and you take your chances I'll pick you up in October or just before freeze-up. I have never left anyone stranded before so you can trust me."

"By the way, you don't know anyone, maybe a young lad that could use that van outside? I won't be needing it anymore so I'll sign off the ownership card and you can keep it or give it away".

The altimeter showed they were flying at 2,500 feet at a speed of 120 miles per hour. The Cessna float plane roared laboriously in a north-bound direction. The sky was blue with little puffs of white clouds above them. Tim had never seen anything like the view he was experiencing. The date was May 15th and there were still little pockets of snow lying on the shady side of hills but the snow was losing its battle with the warming spring sun. Out-of-the-wind stubborn patches of gray-black ice remained in sheltered coves

Ace would occasionally look at a map resting on his lap, look at the compass and then slightly alter his flight path. After they left the seaport, below them were little dirt roads going in various directions with frame homes and farms scattered in the countryside. Occasionally there was a long road which traveled towards the horizon and Ace yelled over the engine noise, "Those are logging roads. They cut mostly black spruce and jack pine." A few small stands of white birch stood out in the green landscape, mostly on hillsides. The scenery was mesmerizing. Small creeks wandered in and out of many lakes. Bogs, marshes and quagmire appeared in view and then disappeared under the wing of the plane. At first there were a few landlocked cottages and some little buildings which Ace said were fly-in hunt camps. It was hard to believe there were so many lakes. They were everywhere sparkling in the mid-day sunshine. Tim yelled at Ace, "There are so many different lakes, how do you find my lake?" Ace smiled. "Every lake has a different shape and after a lot of flying, a pilot recognizes each lake. I guess we are just like you city guys. You know where all the streets and buildings are and we know the same thing here in the bush." Finally, Ace looked at Tim and said,

"I'm starting to drop. See that lake ahead of us? That's where you are going. Do you want me to make a circle around the lake so you can get an idea of the landscape? That little creek going eastward travels to other lakes and probably wanders towards James Bay but I'm not sure, since I've never followed it that far. We're going to land in the middle of the lake and then taxi towards that sand beach. Before we land, I just want to look and see if there are any floating logs or deadheads in the lake. If a pontoon hits a rock or log, they cost a small fortune to replace." Ace circled the lake just skimming above the water, then satisfied, he climbed for some altitude and then dropped on the lake with a gentle bounce and a small spray. When the pontoons could be heard rubbing the sandy beach, the engine was cut and Ace clambered down to the pontoon, untied the canoe said, "Okay, let's start unloading. There were mounds of gear and Ace commented, "I've never seen so much camping equipment for one person in my life."

After they had unloaded Ace said, "Well, greenhorn, good-luck. I'll do a fly-by in a couple of weeks."

For some reason, Tim said, "Do those float planes ever fly upside down or could they ever do a loop d' loop?"

"That's a funny thing to ask. Whatever made you think of that question? Nope, I've never known of anyone to fly upside down. It's because of the pontoons. The plane would lose its stability. I don't know. Maybe it could be done."

"Listen pal, I've got to go to get back before dark. Again, goodluck." Pushing on the wing the plane was turned around, and he started the engine. Listening to the roar, Tim reckoned that Ace had the plane at full throttle as he headed into a mild west wind. It was almost at the end of the lake when the little craft suddenly lifted and just barely cleared the spruce trees. Tim watched the plane grow smaller and smaller, became a little speck and then, to his amazement, the aircraft's nose suddenly pointed upwards into the sky, the pontoons upside-down. Suddenly it dove straight down earthbound. In the horizon, Tim watched a huge black bellow of smoke appear in the sky followed by a distant explosion.

He stared in utter amazement. As the smoke slowly dissolved, only blue sky could be seen. It was unbelievable. Ace had crashed. He had talked to him only a few moments ago. He stood and stared. Finally, he said out loud, "God bless your soul. I hope it was a quick death."

Everything was silent around him. There were no waves lapping the shoreline, the wind was still and no birds sang. Nature maybe was giving Ace a brief requiem.

He found his little camp chair, poured himself some whiskey, mixed it with lake water and lit a cigar. As he stared across the lake, he remembered an old saying, "nature doesn't care if you live or die." He thought to himself, "I hope nature will offer some benevolence and charity to me; a freshman wilderness intruder."

He was depressed. Ace had probably died because of his suggestion about flying the float plane upside down. He had bribed Ace not to enter his location in the log book so no one knew he was living in the wilderness. He had committed crimes against several financial institutions and he knew they would be trying to catch him and have him serve jail time. As the afternoon disappeared, he found his tent boxed with pegs, rods and tent poles. After several mistakes and fumbling with the shelter, it finally was raised. The sun was setting and Tim had another whiskey, watched the sun disappear in the west, found his sleeping bag and went to sleep without supper. He slept exceptionally sound. In the morning as dawn was breaking, he woke to a cacophony of sounds. Red squirrels chattered at possible enemies, ravens croaked as they flew looking for a breakfast of a dead carcass and there were sweet sounds from unknown birds.

He apprehensively un-zipped his tent door and gazed around his camp site. He wondered about the possibility of wolves, bears or some other danger. Seeing none, he decided to examine his gear. With no refrigeration, he knew he should eat the fresh food first before it rotted and he separated that food from the large supply of dried foods. He hoped there would be fish in the lake and possibly he could catch a rabbit or squirrel.

The pile of supplies was huge. With a check-list, he found an axe, fishing equipment, two paddles, clothes for hot, cold, wet and dry weather, a lantern, flashlight, spare batteries, a two burner naphtha cook stove and two gallons of naphtha, pieces of plastic, ten rolls of toilet paper, a signal mirror, sewing kit, band-aids, tobacco and roll-your-own cigarette paper, three bottles of rum and three of rye whiskey, nails, fine wire, a carving knife and a large supply of dried foods plus fresh food inside coolers with ice. For cooking he had one saucepan, fry pan, a pot and some cutlery. He had also bought a small 410 gauge shotgun and two dozen shells. There were several sizes of rope, a fluorescence orange spray bomb, a compass and several containers of matches in a keep-dry container.

At noon, he ate a t-bone steak with mushrooms and onions and enjoyed a cup of black coffee. In the afternoon, he went swimming in the nude and built a crude table out of small saplings. That night, he ate two hot dogs with a soft drink. His new world seemed surreal and while watching the stars that night, he wondered about his mental and physical capabilities for the next few months.

The next day, he trenched around the tent for the run-off of the spring rainstorms he knew would arrive and then re-pegged the base for high winds. He didn't like his crude table and for the rest of the day he re-constructed a bigger, smoother and firmer table tied together with nails and wire. His cutlery was hung on the upright legs. Everything was ready for the next meal and he looked at his creation with admiration.

That night, sitting at his camp fire, he was content but uneasy. He said out loud, "what can harm me?" His mind turned to wolves, cougars, bears, snakes and moose. He wished he had done more research on these animals. Were they nocturnal, daytime animals or both? Would they see him as a threat to their existence or just their next meal? Were they shy or bold? Even the little animals might cause him injury. He knew that fox, skunks and other animals went crazy if they were rabid. He wondered about contaminated water, dental problems or illness. There was no one to help him.

The depression suddenly lifted and he said to himself, "I won't permit fear or anger. I won't worry. I'll accept any bad luck that comes my way with as much bravery as I can muster." He smoked another cigar and congratulated himself on his new-found resolution and rationalization. He went to bed contented.

The next morning, with still a good supply of fresh food, he had fried potatoes, bacon, toast and strong coffee. He stared at the lake and thought, "I might as well see if I can catch a fish, that is, if there are any fish in the lake."

Tim paddled out in the lake about two hundred yards. He had read that lake trout like deep cold water. A silver spoon was hooked on the snap swivel which was attached to the line. The wind slowly drifted the canoe down the lake. He peeled off line until he felt the lure strike the bottom and he pulled it up he reckoned about two feet. He jigged the lure to give it movement and about ten minutes later, there were three hard jerks, his rod bent and line screamed off the reel. The fish was a fighter. It shook its head back and forth, then sulked on the bottom. At first there was no winner but Tim constantly raised and lowered the rod and the fish slowly yielded to the pressure and finally reached the surface. It was a dandy; Tim guessed about seven pounds, the largest fish he had ever caught. He cautiously slipped his fingers under the gill and flipped it into the canoe. He fished for two more hours and caught nothing more.

That night, he sat at his new table, ate the golden fish filet, fried potatoes, boiled corn and washed it down with a can of beer. "Not bad for a greenhorn." he said.

He decided not to clean his dishes until the next morning, lit a cigar and watched the sunset and night sky. He wished he had studied more astronomy. The sky sparkled and blinked from horizon to horizon with planets, stars or both. The immensity of the heavens was over-whelming. Several times he saw a shooting star flash across the sky and disappear. He added more sticks and roots to his campfire which caused sparks to fly upwards into the night. It was a night most city people would never experience.

Occasionally loons on the lake would give their mournful calls back and forth to one another and unseen night birds could be heard calling. For a while an owl hooted in the distance and then stopped and Tim surmised it probably had caught some small nocturnal animal that had become careless around the bird known as "the silent night killer."

Around midnight he decided to have one more cigar. His mind wandered around about the creation of God and eternity. He thought about the death of Ace and wondered about his spirit's destination after the crash.

Tim had a restless night with his thoughts flipping from one problem to another. He wondered if any of his embezzled targets or the police were looking for him yet. He knew that he would have to devise a scheme to get out of the bush. God! Maybe he would never get out. He thought about dying from starvation or freezing to death and he knew he could not survive a winter. He did believe that to gain an inner peace, he must be in communion with nature but he also knew the truism that many adventures are frightful. He remembered one explorer had said, "It's just an adventure. Don't try and justify it. It's just an adventure."

In the morning, he ate the other lake trout filet and decided he should try and have a project every day. He reasoned it was no good to be idle as time would pass too slowly and boredom would be dangerous to his mental and physical well-being.

CHAPTER 5

EXCERPTS FROM THE DIARY OF TIM McKAY

Dear Diary:

To-day, the first part of June is the start of my new project. I'm nervous of the thick bush but I've been going into the woods, (not very far) to defecate and urinate and I realize this can't continue.

I cleared a short trail by cutting the underbrush, low hanging limbs and brushing a path about 50 feet to the east side of my tent-site. With my camp shovel, I dug a hole about five foot deep and the length and width was about two feet. This took me all day because of tree roots growing in every direction underground. The next day I cut logs and that took all day. (I wish I had a chain saw). The logs were laid on the ground where they formed three sides, about 15" high. A lower log on the fourth side is where I sit and I shaved it smooth, (the best I could) with my camp axe to avoid getting slivers in my rear end. It will be a little spooky to walk through the bush to use this new toilet in the dark but I will conserve my flashlight batteries. If I have *"to go"*, I'll try and do it in the day time. (If my friends could see me trying to make a homemade latrine, they would be holding their sides with laughter)

· ·

I have lost track of the date but know it is around the end of June. I had read about black flies but had no idea they can be so bad and fierce. They have arrived in clouds and they bite anywhere there is exposed flesh. They try to crawl up my nose, get inside my ears, creep under my clothes and they love to bite where my hairline meets my neck. They could cause a person who is lost in the woods to go crazy. One solution is to have a good fire with lots of smoke so I sit, down-wind, with the smoke blowing on me. The trick getting bellows of smoke is to place green boughs on the hot embers. I tuck my stockings over my pant cuffs, wear a hooded sweater and gloves. I have elastic bands over my clothing at the wrists. They are quite small and there is some relief on windy days as they are not good flyers. I have sometimes smeared mud on my face and this stops some of them from biting. I can't imagine how wild animals can tolerate these nasty creatures as they will actually crawl in your eyes. I think they will be gone in a couple or three weeks. It has been said that some people living in the north are not bothered by these little monsters. I wonder how that could be?

· ·

The black flies have subsided a lot. Sometime around the middle of June the clouds of mosquitoes arrived. The black flies bite and the mosquitoes sting. I take the same preventive measures for them. Sometimes, I go out in the lake where they don't seem to bother me and I just float around the lake in the canoe. They are most annoying if they get inside the tent as they buzz and hum. I once read that only female mosquitoes sting as they want blood for breeding purposes. I must say there are a hell of a lot of sexy females trying to sting me! I should have asked Victor Tobiah for more money to compensate me for the agony I'm getting from all these cruel insects! Few city people would realize the hoards of them!

. . . .

Most of these diary entries are mundane so I don't write every day. I am out of fresh food but the dried dehydrated food is surprisingly good. I usually tidy my tent, clean my little beach of any debris that might have floated in during the night, wash clothes in the lake and almost every day, I collect wood.

In the beginning, there were a lot of dry sticks, branches and roots around the campsite but they have all been collected and burned. Now, I travel around the shoreline in the canoe and collect dry wood that has been thrown up on the shore by wind and waves. I discovered early that green wood does not burn. I usually have a low burning fire all day long. There is something comforting about a fire, particularly at night.

To-day while patrolling, I found some large roots along the shoreline that I managed to drag into the canoe. On the same trip I found a good supply of sun-dried sticks and logs. The canoe was over-loaded and had settled low in the water. For some reason, I carelessly turned around, lost my balance and the canoe turned upside down. Part of the canoe or a log banged me on the head and momentarily I was stunned and went under the water. I took in a mouthful of water, gagged, then kicked as hard as I could and broke upward to the lake surface. My clothes and shoes became waterlogged and I went under again. This time I held my breath.

When I came up for the second time, my collected wood was floating all around me and the canoe was starting to drift away with the wind. I knew I would drown if I didn't catch the canoe. Because of the distance, it was impossible for me to swim to shore. I swam with every bit of energy in my body and caught the overturned canoe. I rested for a while, reached under the water, caught the gunnel and slowly managed to turn it right-side-up. At least I wasn't going to die. Kicking, I pushed it full of water towards shore and about one hour later, I landed exhausted and collapsed on the beach. I eventually changed into dry clothes and hung my wet clothes on a line over the drying fire. I remembered an old wilderness saying, "Having survival skills is important, having the will to survive is essential."

. . . .

I'm sure it is early August. I've seen summer storms with severe lightning bolts flashing close to my camp site. No wild animals have bothered me but I did see a moose or caribou track along my little beach that was made in the night The whiskey jack birds keep coming around looking for a food handout., I figure my food supply could last another month with some rationing, Luckily, my tent did not leak during some wicked rain storms. I have read all my ten books and may start again. My stay here has been a long lonesome ordeal. I wonder how hermits and society recluses can handle a solitary existence?

One book I want to write about in my diary is called, "Field Guide to Mammals." It is not a story, just an encyclopedia/documentation about North American animals, written by numerous researchers and people belonging to the Society of Mammalogy. A few things intrigued me. Why there is such a variation in animal behavior? Basically, an animal wants three things; to reproduce for the continuation of the species, to have food and to survive. Darwin, around 1859, wrote that species will always change by natural selection. My question is: why have animals not chosen a common method to survive? The huge polar and grizzly bear add around 400 pounds just before winter and then hibernate until spring. They even have their little off-springs while sleeping. The little artic fox stays awake all winter and tries to find little scraps of food. Why doesn't it hibernate? The woodchuck/groundhog also goes into hibernation and it's body temperature drops to 4

Celsius and has a heartbeat of 4 per minute. Why doesn't the coyote, deer or wolf do this? The little brown weasel turns white in the wintertime (then called ermine) for disguise purposes and the snowshoe rabbit does the same thing. Why not the raccoon or porcupine? Has one species found the secret of survival by changing colors?

Well, diary, it is still pouring rain so I'm going to continue with this subject.

The frail monarch butterfly takes the perilous journey each fall to Mexico. Is there not a shorter flying place in California or Florida? Why don't other butterflies make the same journey? Which one will survive?

Dozens of bird species go south every winter yet the chickadee, woodpecker, nuthatch and grouse don't leave the north. It is reported that there are 1,326 species of mice and rats in the world. Why is there such a huge population when other species are not surviving?

Is there a grand heavenly plan for the continuation of certain species or was Darwin right saying it the "survival of the fittest?

In evolution, some species were water animals but now are on land. Others, like the marine iguanas are returning to the sea.

Diary, I'm going to quit writing about these observations because I don't have the answers. It is obvious that each species has an inherent plan for their continuation but some obviously will be wrong.

Adolph Hitler thought the species he called "The Arian Race" should rule the world but, much to his dismay, the rest of the world disagreed.

I have no conclusions why animals change or disappear but I sure as hell will not be reading "A Field Guide On Insects." as the mammals still baffle me.

CHAPTER 6

LIFE AT THE CAMPSITE

At the campsite most nights, Tim considered all the precautions he had taken to avoid detection. He reckoned there was not much more he could have done but he knew the Police would make every effort to catch him. The consequences of getting caught would be devastating. A trial, jail time, a fine, community service work, newspaper publicity, an embarrassment to his family and friends, the end of his profitable lecturing career and no future bank credit or financial relationships with any loaning institutions. Maybe he should have thought of the consequences before making such a deal with Victor Tobiah.

Tim McKay had no previous history of criminal activities and he thought the Police would have a hard time connecting him with Larry Johnson who had now disappeared. D.N.A. evidence could be the most damaging and Tim had done exhaustive studies on their results.

He knew the banks had many video pictures of Larry Johnson and also that the Police would know he had been in disguise. He hoped his trickery was good enough to fool the bank experts. They would be well aware he had been disguised and would try to re-construct his appearance. Saliva, blood, perspiration, semen and other body fluids could be used for identification but Tim was positive the police would not find any of his liquids. Camera eye technology was being used for the retina and iris but Tim thought the banks had not yet installed this sophisticated equipment. Other new methods were camera ear prints, shoe prints, the old stand-by fingerprints and hand writing comparisons by graphologists.

The apartment had been cleaned and double cleaned. He had worn surgical gloves and a paste on his fingertips when in the apartment. He knew hair particles got in the sink and toilet drains and he had used a plumber's acid for a clean-out. His shoes were removed each time he entered the apartment and each time he had changed to plain sole slippers which eventually would be destroyed.

Victor Tobiah was the only person who knew a Tim McKay had committed crimes but Tim thought it unlikely he would expose him to the Police since Tobiah had a huge bet to collect from the Eastern Ontario Better's Club. Tobiah had assured him that the members of this betting club would not be told the name of the embezzler but who knew his truthfulness?

Ethel Grant of Texas had seen him transformed but she had known him as Harry Bennett of Corpus Christie. He doubted if the Canadian investigators would connect Harry Bennett to Larry Johnson to Tim McKay. It would be a long reach. His disguise purchases had been made at several places between Texas and the Canadian border and they had been made in such small quantities so not to alarm the vendors. He had paid cash and they had not asked his name. He did wonder if the American Police might be curious about a person wanting to change his looks, especially with their paranoia terrorist worries.

All of his disguises had been burned over two hundred miles away at a campsite on his trip north. The old van had been purchased under a false name and then given away at the seaport terminal. He knew his huge purchase of camping equipment might tip off the Police that someone was going into the bush for an extended period and he had bought some in the States, some in Toronto and the balance from many stores as he proceeded north.

From his campsite, he could see a small stand of white birch trees and their leaves had started to turn their autumn bright yellow. Tim calculated it was about the second week of September. Camping alone was a paradox. There was the peacefulness of existence yet an uneasiness. He had been a type A personality with a quickness of thought and activity and the solitary life was the antithesis of his previous life. He was experiencing an un-sought tranquility. He continued to wonder how hermits and trappers solved their solitary life style.

During the Spring rainstorms, he had been a recluse in his tent until he realized a roof could be built over his little table. With four corner saplings and a plastic tarpaulin cover he now actually enjoyed watching the storms come and go.

He had written in his diary:

"Last night, a pack of wolves could be heard rapidly approaching my tent. They were howling and I guess they were probably chasing a deer. Suddenly, there was a loud splash at the water's edge and the wolves became silent. I guess their quarry saved his or her life using the lake as a refuge."

"Another interesting thing took place. A large gull was pouncing on the water, rising up and then dropping and striking something on the surface of the lake. I took the canoe to see what the commotion was about and found a little red squirrel swimming and the gull was constantly pecking at it. I could see some blood on the squirrel's head and when I arrived, the ring-billed gull flew away figuring I was too formidable a foe. The little squirrel finally made shore and before entering the bush, it looked at me and I swear its eyes said "thank-you." End of diary for today.

Tim tried to find different things to do each day. He started carving and produced some surprising results with a little wooden fish being his best creation. He had forgotten a razor, a mirror and a comb and realized his appearance must be terrible with a shaggy beard and long scraggly hair. He decided to try shaving with his fillet knife but it was too painful.

He had seen knife throwing contests on t.v. so he made a target, stood back ten paces and began practicing. It took a long time, most of an afternoon, but to his satisfaction, he eventually hit his target every time.

Each afternoon, he did his wood searching job. It was comforting to have a good supply at his tent site. When at the far side of the lake he had pulled his canoe high on shore to prevent it drifting away and while holding an armful of sticks and logs, he looked up and to his amazement, a red canoe was crossing the lake, heading for his campsite. After almost four months of solitary living, the sight startled him. For a while he stared at the lone paddler. He was un-decided about hiding for a while or confronting the person. He watched the person walk around his campsite and then sit in his camp chair. He waited about thirty minutes and then started across the lake with some trepidation.

CHAPTER 7

MARION HENRY

Marion's mother Julie Henry had been one of many Indian children who were forced to leave their community and live in a residential home. The Government of Canada, The Roman Catholic Church, The Anglican Church of Canada and The Presbyterian Church of Canada participated in this venture where over 150,000 children were taken from their homes and forced to assimilate into the world of the 'white man'. At most schools, the experiment resulted in cultural genocide. The idea was to take the 'Indian' out of the child.

Many of these children were beaten, forbidden to speak their native language, terrorized, starved, sexually and physically abused. Most of the programmes were closed down in the 1970's and the last school shut in 1984. By 2007, there were over 5,000 lawsuits against the Government and Churches which represented 12,000 Indians and it was estimated there would be a settlement of about $24,000 per person with a total settlement of $1.9 billion. Varying amounts were given depending on their circumstances and proof of claim. Some of the financial offers were refused which led to more expenses through litigation.

When they were permitted to return to their Indian villages, many of the residential people turned to alcohol, some committed suicide, many had lost their ability to earn a living and there was a lot of abuse from the men towards their wives and children. Julie Henry had had a difficult marriage to a man who became an alcoholic and eventually died. During the time of the marriage, she had one daughter, Marion. Mother Julie was determined that her daughter would have a chance at an education and when she was a teenager, Marion agreed to live with a relative in Calgary where she finished high school, went to University, got her Bachelor of Arts, a Masters Degree in criminal work and learned how to speak French. Julie paid part of the costs with money from the residential home settlement and the Provincial and Federal Government gave generous grants.

The Royal Canadian Mounted Police had watched her progress in university and felt she would be an asset to the Force. Other places also offered a job but she liked the prospect of working in the northern parts of Canada. She had a variety of jobs including traffic, criminal investigations, search and rescue, drug busts and white collar crimes. Marion finally reached enough seniority where she received one month's holidays. Her mother's village had a battery radio and once a week Marion called her mother at a prescribed time. This time, her mother complained of a fever, nighttime chills, loss of appetite and there was no doubt she was seriously ill. In addition to her regular holidays, Marion requested and was granted compassionate leave for an extra month with the condition she spend a portion of the month in undercover work in the Town of Hearst as the Mounties had received some reports of soft drugs being sold in that area.

An exploration company flew regular flights near the James Bay area and Marion arranged to hitch a ride to her hometown of Ogoki on the Albany River. She found her mother bed-ridden, dehydrated with a fever and Marion promptly called for a nurse or Doctor to fly in to their town. A Practical Nurse diagnosed the illness as influenza type A and had Julie flown to a hospital in Cochrane where she was placed in isolation and began receiving treatments. Marion decided to start her undercover work in Hearst while waiting for Julie's recovery.

An Indian woman sat at the end of the bar, dressed in cheap clothing, giving the appearance of another Indian who had left a reservation and was living on welfare, probably another alcoholic. The bartender had been quietly called and told that whenever she ordered a beer, it was to be a soft drink and after his quizzical argumentative look, she flashed her badge and told him not to mention it to anyone. Occasionally, a man would approach her and ask her how much she charged for sex, preferably a blow job. She told them she was not interested and for them not to continue badgering her, she said, "leave me alone or I'll cut off your penis with my knife." They scurried away and told their friends to stay away from her.

At the bar, two pilots were getting drunk after they had finished their flying schedules for the day. Marion listened to their conversation.

"That was a strange thing about Ace. They know he took off with some guy with a load of camping gear but he never logged his flight."

"Yup, he must have crashed but even after searching, nothing ever turned up. Of course, the search problem was, no one knew exactly where to look for the crash site. Geez, every plane around here looked for him. I wonder who the guy was that hired him?"

"That damned bush is so thick that maybe no one will ever find him. He was a good pilot. Funny thing he didn't record his flight. I wonder if his passenger went down with him. Maybe he had dropped the guy off and was returning home I guess we will never know. Maybe his passenger is still up there somewhere in the bush."

Marion was curious about the conversation but plane crashing and lost pilots were not in her instructions unless drugs were involved.

Marion's mother was finally home and getting better. Marion told her mother she had decided to go on a lone canoe trip for a couple of weeks and maybe do some trapping. Secretly, she really wanted to get back to the old Indian ways of living off the land. The price for beaver, mink, muskrat, marten and fox pelts were high and she figured her mother could use some extra money. After she returned, she thought she might try for a moose or caribou kill. It would give the villagers some meat for the winter and they could make moccasins and some clothing from the hides.

After three days of paddling, finding trap sites and camping, she had seen no one in the wilderness and now was amazed to see a green tent on a sandy beach at an isolated lake. At the campsite, there were still warm embers in the fire pit and some clothes hanging on a line. She decided to wait and soon, a canoe appeared, riding low in the water filled with wood. When it landed, a fellow with a beard and long hair stared at her and finally said simply, "hello." She responded her "hello" and then started helping by carrying the wood from the canoe to the existing pile.

After that chore was done, she said, "You sure surprised me when I saw your tent. What are you doing here? Tim gave his rehearsed story, "I'm an outdoor writer for a magazine in Rochester, New York, and we are trying an experiment of a greenhorn living, or attempting to live alone in the bush. As you can see," he added, "so far, I'm still alive." and he gave a big grin.

"And you, I'm just as surprised to see a woman traveling in this wilderness by herself. What's your story?"

Marion replied, "I'm part of an Indian tribe and I'm getting ready for the trapping season, trying to find places to set my traps for beaver, muskrat and other animals with fur. Do you want a cup of Indian tea?"

"Sure, what is Indian tea?"

"You take leaves from a young strawberry plant, dry them by a fire and let them steep a little longer than regular tea." Tim found the taste a little bitter but satisfying.

The two of them sat, sipped their tea and said nothing for a long time. She finally said, "I don't know your name, what is it?" and he replied, "Jim Johnson, but everybody calls me Jimmy. And what's yours." She answered, "Marion Young." and he continued, "how did you get here." Marion said, "I've been traveling for over three days. At night I cut some saplings, make an

A frame shelter with a tarpaulin roof and then I cut some evergreen boughs to sleep on, cover them with a piece of canvass and lay under a Hudson Bay blanket. I catch a few fish, trap an occasional rabbit plus I carry some dried meats and wild vegetables. I have a twelve gauge shotgun and I shoot a duck or goose if I can get close enough and there are lots of grouse in the bush that are easy to catch. It's a great life and I enjoy it."

In the late afternoon, Tim said, "would you like to try some of my dried foods for dinner? I've got beef jerky, mashed potatoes and vegetables. Everything is dehydrated and water has to be added. I don't have any fresh food but the dried food is quite tasty." Marion said, "Sure, thanks for asking me."

They sat after supper sipping Tim's tea, the sun was slowly setting and she said, "Jimmy, do you mind if I stay here for a few days? I can teach you some things about the bush, fishing and trapping, that is, if you want to learn some of the Indian's way of surviving in the wilderness."

The name Jimmy surprised him. He thought, "My God, now I've got to remember another name." He answered, "Sure, I'd like to see Indian cooking and trapping. You should know that I've never killed or cleaned an animal."

She replied, "I'll show you some stuff but now, I'll take some of my gear into your tent."

Tim thought, "Geez, is she thinking about sex?", but he reckoned that, he should wait for a signal, hint or invitation before he did anything stupid. He gave her the courtesy of getting modestly un-dressed and when he went into the tent that night, she was curled up against the far wall under her blanket and her gear and equipment in the middle of the tent formed a barrier between them.

CHAPTER 8

JIMMY'S EDUCATION

He wakened at the song of the first morning bird. Marion had left the tent and Tim smelled coffee. She had prepared a breakfast of powdered pancakes and scrambled eggs. It was a real treat to have someone cook his breakfast for him.

It was a bright early fall morning and Marion said, "Would you like to live like an Indian to-day?" Tim said, "Yes" and she added, "we'll start after I have a swim." Tim lit one of his few remaining cigars and watched her go in the lake with a modest bathing suit but he couldn't help but notice her superb physical condition. It crossed his mind that a man wouldn't want to trifle with her apparent strength. It was also obvious that she did some body building. He wondered if she was who she claimed to be plus he had noticed she was highly intelligent.

She dressed in khakis, both pants and top and Tim could see that they were recently purchased. Something seemed amiss with her story but maybe she would accidentally give away some information

She asked, "If you were really hungry, would you eat a rat or a mouse?" He replied, "It isn't exactly my choice for a meal but I guess if a person is hungry enough, anything edible would do to avoid starvation."

She nodded her head yes and told him to watch her. She found a flat rock, placed it on its edge and let it lean propped by a little stick. A piece of left-over pancake was placed under the rock with a string attached from the bait to the stick. Marion said, "Look, when I move the bait, the rock will fall, crushing the small animal and hopefully killing it. Now let me see you do it except this time, balance a heavy log on its end prop it up with the stick and do the same with the string and the bait." Tim tried it several times but the balancing act with the log was tricky as it kept toppling over. He finally got Marion's approval. They left the balanced rock and the log and she said they would check it later. Marion added, "Always try and find a tiny path where the animals might travel. The trap usually crushes them during the night when they are out scavenging for food. Sometimes a larger animal like a fox, marten or mink might trip the trap but they can escape. I have occasionally caught a snake or a toad but I have been told toads are poisonous. This method of catching small animals is called deadfall traps and they can often make the difference for a person's survival."

"Okay, let's find a birch tree, if we can." He followed her along the shoreline, found a clump of birch trees and she took her knife and peeled off a sheet of the white bark. It was almost like paper. She rolled it up until it was coned shaped and then filled it with water and placed it on a fire until it boiled. "Never drink water out in the bush unless you have boiled it first. There is a bacteria called giardia and it comes usually from beaver fecal matter. You can boil water in a hat, a sardine tin or anything you have that will hold water. This giardia has infectious microscopic organisms in it. Sometimes it gets there from birds or animals and it can even come from humans in a populated area. Some people add iodine to their water but boiling is the best solution. You can buy pills that will purify water but remember, even if the water looks clean, don't trust it. The symptoms are diarrhea, stomach cramps and belching. One fellow that caught it said he could shoot further out his rear end than his front. The common name is beaver's disease."

That afternoon, she said, "You go and get some wood. I shot a duck the other day and we can have it for supper. I already pulled the guts so it wouldn't spoil and I'll take off the feathers while you are gone." When he left in the canoe, Marion went in the tent and, with a policeman's caution; she looked in his gear for any information about Jimmy. She had not believed he was an outdoor writer. She did find a simple road map and a thousand dollars. There were no note pads usual to a writer's custom of making notes. She was sure he had lied about his occupation.

That night, after supper, she talked to him about survival in the bush. Marion said that the older Indians had taught her quite a bit about the bush and she had read a book about the psychology of survival. "Some people get a little crazy if they think they are lost. When they are lost over twenty-four hours, they get depressed. Then, they get angry. Quite often they deny they are lost and start wandering around, sometimes in big circles. When they realize their situation is hopeless, they often start bargaining with a higher authority, like God, to guide them to safety. Finally, they sometime just lie down and accept the fact they are going to die and occasionally they do. If you are lost, avoid fear and anxiety as that can be your worst enemy. Sit down, take a few deep breaths and if you have water, drink some of it because you will think more clearly if you are hydrated. Try and stay where you are because most times, someone will find you. Study and then remember that there are a lot of bush survival techniques, mainly shelter, water, food and fire. Signal fires are great if you hear an aircraft. That night they talked very little and instead, watched the fire throw off its upward sparks and viewed the amazing sky with the twinkling stars and a huge moon. Before going to bed, she said, "I can show you quite a bit more of the bush including snares and wild food. That is, if you want to learn some more." Tim nodded his head and replied, "Yup, that would be great, especially for my outdoor writing."

When he went to bed, Marion was snuggled on her side of the tent. He realized he should gain as much knowledge from her as possible in case he had to travel or spend some extra time in the bush. After she left his campsite, he would prepare three bundles of wood on the beach for a signal fire and also place a stick with a white cloth out in the water. Surely a sea-plane would fly over the vicinity of his camp site sometime.

She again was up early and they had a simple breakfast of bannock. She said, the first thing we will do is go fishing. He decided not to tell her he already was a successful fisherman and with naïve pretence, he climbed in the canoe with her. She used only a hand-line with a silver lure. She told Tim to paddle very, very slowly as she jigged the bait off the lake bottom. Moments later she flipped a laker into the canoe. "I guess you don't need any fishing lessons, this place has lots of fish" and they returned to the campsite. She ripped open the stomach, removed the head, gills, fins and tail and threw them into the lake. "With a lake trout, there are no scales and the skin is quite tasty. She explained the unwanted parts would be eaten by crabs, gulls and crayfish within a day.

The next thing was going into the bush. "If you have a compass, bring it. Also, bring some fine wire. Start walking north and I'll follow you."

The walking was hard. They had a spongy moss under-footing, spruce branches that intertwined, fallen trees and logs to climb over and some wet bogs to go around. After thirty minutes, she said, "Okay, turn around and walk back to the tent." He used the compass and went due south but he arrived at the lake about one hundred yards from his tent-site. Marion said, "not good enough, start again, but this time make an observation where the sun is, if there are any unusual large trees, which way the water flowed when crossing a creek, any small hills that you walk over and how wide the beaver dam was. So tell me what you see as we walk. Tim told her what he was seeing and after forty-five minutes, she said, "o.k." turn around and go back." The sun had been over his right shoulder so he reversed it's location and commented to her things he remembered. He still looked at his compass from time to time. Sometimes they walked in a semicircle to avoid a bog and one beaver dam led them in a north-east direction. He corrected the twists and turns with some guidance from Marion and this time they arrived at the lake about twenty five yards from the tent. She said, "much better, Jimmy, but still not good enough for the bush."

It was noon-hour and while Marion slow roasted the lake trout on a spit above the red coals Tim created some scalloped potatoes from a dried food recipe. That afternoon, Marion told him about snares with the thin wire.

"Listen, do you hear that squirrel chattering." She followed the sound and found the little creature on a branch scolding them for their intrusion. Marion said, "I'll walk to the opposite side of the tree and tie a snare on the tree trunk." When she was done, she startled the squirrel and it scampered down away from their view. The loop entrapped the little animal and the snare tightened as it struggled. Marion took a stick, hit it over the head. It shuddered once and died. She removed the head, tail and guts, skinned it and wiped the blood with some green moss.

"We'll wash the carcass at the lake" and she put the small piece of meat in her jacket pocket.

The next squirrel was heard and Tim set the snare with Marion's guidance. The same technique was used and Tim stared at the struggling animal. She said, "Jimmy, for God's sake, kill it. Don't ever permit an animal to suffer." It died with the first blow of the stick. "Don't let the blood and guts bother you or you will never eat in the wilderness." Tim had his first experience preparing an animal for food.

On their return to the campsite, Marion found some curly green fiddleheads growing in an open spot. "We will clean them then boil them with some salt. That night they ate a "bush dinner" of roasted squirrel and fried fiddleheads. Tim said, "That was a delicious meal," and he ate until none remained.

Just before dark, Marion said, "we'll set some ground snares for rabbits." Three snares were set nearby the camp site. They then checked the deadfall traps and under the rock, one mouse had been killed. Marion made him clean the mouse much to his objection and a tiny bit of meat was recovered.

Marion said, "We can use it for bait at a deadfall or you can eat it. It actually tastes pretty good after cooking if you are lost and hungry."

That night they talked about religion, the planets, stars and mysteries. Both of them were tired and went to bed early. Tim again gave her the modesty of going to bed first.

At dawn, he again smelled coffee. They ate a breakfast of cold duck and some greens

"Do you want me to show you some more survival things or have you had enough?"

"No, I find it really interesting and I'll appreciate knowing more about your Indian lore."

Marion said, "Okay, let's get started. There is a little marsh at the end of the lake so we'll go there first." They stopped where a bunch of cattails were growing. "At the top, there is the pollen part and it makes for good eating. Below is the fluffy part inside that brown thing which looks like corn on the cob. You can eat it if it isn't too old. Then, pull the cattails out by the roots. You can chew the root cores after peeling away the outside layers.

While paddling back to the camp she said, "You will find mushrooms once in a while but my advice to you is, DON'T EAT THEM. If you make a mistake and eat a toxic mushroom, they can kill you. It is said there are old mushroom hunters, and then there are bold mushroom hunters-but there are no old, bold mushroom hunters.

If you look on the water, you can eat water lilies, reed grass and bull rushes, but, if you are not sure, don't eat them."

When in the bush, you won't find much to eat in the swampy places but on higher ground, you might find chokecherries beside a stream but only eat them when they are dark, purple-black. On higher ground you can eat the inside of the milkweed pod and the shoots that taste like asparagus and should be boiled. On the ground, you can find blueberries, wild strawberries and raspberries. But, Jimmy, don't get caught here in the wintertime. You probably wouldn't survive. The ice will be three foot thick, the air often well below zero, the wildlife becomes scarce and you cannot travel without a snowmobile or a dog sled. Get the hell out of here when you have the chance. Did you notice there is a little color change in the leaves? Winter comes early and stays late."

That night, Marion said, "I'm leaving tomorrow morning to continue checking my trapping places. When I come back about three days from now, can I stay here with you?"

"Sure, I'll be glad to see you again."

They were quiet for a while, watching the sky spectacle and the sparks shooting from the fire. Marion asked, "by the way, how much were you charged for the seaplane trip here and back?" Tim replied too quickly, "Ace asked me for a thousand dollars but he took less."

She jerked her head towards Tim, "Did you say Ace was your pilot?

He realized his mistake and said, "No, I should have said Ace quoted me a thousand dollars but I got someone else named Billy to fly me here and he is supposed to get me in a couple of weeks."

Marion said, "Did you know Ace very well?"

He replied, "No, I just got a quick price from him and then Billy and I planned the trip."

Marion said nothing more. She thought, "This guy knows something about Ace. Maybe he killed him. I've got to get a report to the police because something strange has happened and Jimmy isn't telling me the truth."

CHAPTER 9

ADIEU

He had planned to try and make love with Marion that night but surrendered the thought after his mistake about Ace. Her tone of voice had stiffened when Pilot Ace's name had been mentioned. She had stared at Tim momentarily and then became quiet. There was something suspicious about Marion and it unnerved him. When they had discussed politics at the fire last night, she was strangely quiet about any opinions. Tim wondered if, perhaps, the Government was her employer and she was being careful not to step on any toes that would hurt her career.

As he lay in bed he was certain that Marion would report the conversation to someone, probably the Police or some authoritative person. There was no doubt they had searched for Ace without success. In a small populated but vast area, word of mouth about his disappearance would travel fast and Tim was certain that Marion knew the story of Pilot Ace.

Tim knew the process. Marion would tell the Police that Tim had mentioned Ace's name. She would also tell them that a man named Jimmy was living in the bush with no practical outdoor experience and also, she was sure he was not a journalist. The Police would fly in and question him about his identity, his knowledge of Ace and his reasons for being in the bush for several months. They would do a follow-up with his fictitious employer and find his cover story had been false. They would also issue a bulletin to other Police Forces stating there was an unknown man living in the bush with suspicious circumstances about the disappearance and probable death of a bush pilot named Ace. Of course, Police from other communities were always looking for someone who had disappeared after certain unsolved crimes had been committed. This pony-express-electronic message system would take perhaps a week minimum after Marion's report and Tim decided he would not wait. They had not found him yet and they were not going to catch him now.

In the morning after a hasty breakfast, Marion packed her belongings in her canoe and told Tim she would be traveling west for two or three days before returning. He wished her good luck and waved goodbye as she paddled in the still calm of the water. He waited an hour in case she returned.

Tim had made a mental inventory the night before of the equipment and food needed. In his watertight bag went matches, halazone water-purifying tablets, six fish hooks, thirty feet of fishing line, some aluminum foil, tea bags, a pocket knife, fifteen feet of rope, one change of clothing, a rain suit, his bush axe, four days of dried food, a fry pan and sauce pan, some cutlery, a big piece of plastic, compass and a sleeping bag.

One night she had told him of her travels from a little village named Ogoki on the Albany River and one afternoon she had drawn him a map from her little village to his campsite. It was a complicated trip for a greenhorn with twists and turns through rivers and lakes. It was etched in his mind, "nature doesn't care if you live or die" and he knew he would die if he got trapped in a Canadian winter.

When leaving his lake, it was shallow and he pulled some bull-rushes by their roots. He would eat them later. The outlet flowed almost due south and then the small river made an abrupt swing to the north. Twice that day he had encountered small sets of rapids and he was forced to attach his rope to the canoe and lower it over the rocks and eddies. He paddled across another lake and finally reached a junction of another river which went south. It was three in the afternoon, the days were getting shorter and Tim was tired, thirsty and hungry. A small jut of land at the river junction looked like a good campsite and he stopped for the night. With driftwood, he made a fire using one of his precious matches, sterilized some lake water and had tea. Willow trees were cut and an A frame was made then covered with plastic. On the ground he placed evergreen boughs for a cushion and laid out his sleeping bag.

Marion had taught him well. At a rotting stump he got some white grubs, placed them on a fishing hook and tied his line to a shoreline tree. He then rigged a wire snare for any small animal that might pass by and could be entrapped. He ate one of his dried food dinners and boiled the roots of the cattail plant. He decided on one more cup of tea.

His little fire threw white sparks and the small dry driftwood pieces burned a brilliant red before changing to the orange glow of the dying coals. He was watching a bright meteor streaking through the star speckled sky and then a ghostly, faint, milky glow appeared in the northern sky. Slowly it developed into a greenish arc which then formed into a dramatic display of yellow-green-lights. The mixture of lights also had a crimson glow which shot across the heavens, almost from horizon to horizon. Tim watched in amazement as the rapidly changing sky showed veils, arcs and patches. The speed of the flashing lights were astounding as one color after another seemed mixed and then magically disappeared. He had read about this solar event called the aurora borealis but he never had imagined he would see such a dramatic show of light, speed and color. He wished he had had a video camera as he knew he could never adequately explain the overwhelming spectacle he had witnessed. Tim eventually crawled into his new tent and slept until dawn when honking geese flying south awakened him.

His snare was empty but he had caught a little chub on his line which he cleaned and fried. It was enough for two bites and he ate a few wild strawberries found near his camp. The river flowed almost due south, crossing one little pond and then at another junction, it went due east passing three creeks. Tim was concerned he might be making the wrong turns but at the end of the day, a big river flowed. It had to be the Albany River which went eventually to James Bay. Again, he made his camp, set out snares, fishing lines and built a fire. He ate one of his dried dinners, sterilized the water for tea and at dark, happily again watched the beauty of the northern lights. His great grandmother had written a poem and Tim had written some music for it. He sang in the darkness and only the night birds and the stillness of the wilderness heard his song.

There was a boy named Dilly Dall,
Who would not do his work;
He had a pal, named Shilly Shall,
Who also was a shirk."

Said Dilly Dall to Shilly Shall,
"Let's play the whole day through!"
Said Shilly Shall to Dilly Dall,
"That's what I'd like do."

When Dilly Dall became a man,
He had no food to eat;
And, Shilly Shall was just as poor,
And so they begged for meat.

The people said, "we can't feed you,
Why don't you go to work?"

"We don't know how", said Dilly Dall,
"We only learned to shirk."

"If you won't work, then you can't eat,"
The people did reply.
So Dilly Dall and Shilly Shall,
Just laid them down to die.

They slept all day, they slept all night
And when they woke again,
They found their stomachs full of naught,
Their bodies full of pain.

"I say, old pal," groaned Dilly Dall,
"This dying is hard work!"
"I faith your right," sighed Shilly Shall,
"I wonder should we shirk?"

So up they got and went to work
And found at set of sun,
That work well done became to them,
The very best of fun.

The morning temperature was crisp and a mist was rising off the river water, a sure indication of the coming fall. Tim checked his snares and there lay a quivering rabbit, brown and with partially white fur showing it's winter disguise. A single crack over the head with a stick killed the animal. It was skinned, gutted and roasted with a spit over the fire. He could not believe how hungry he had become and he ate most of it. He said out loud, "Marion, I thank you for teaching me."

The canoe was reloaded and he headed westbound on the Albany river. Paddling was slow and tiresome. At noon he spotted some frame houses. Indian children ran to his canoe and stared at him. It was then he realized his appearance must be a mess with long dirty hair to his shoulders, unshaven and un-clean clothes. He tried "kipa'ma" which he hoped was Cree for mother and then "kipa'pa" but they didn't speak. An elderly woman approached his canoe and he tried "at'nsi" which he hoped meant "how are you" in Cree. She only nodded at him and then another woman walked to the shoreline. Tim asked if she spoke English and she said. "Yes". He asked if he was at Ogoki and again she said. "Yes". She asked, "Who are you, where did you come from and can we help you?". He thought he might try some more Cree, "kinana'skmitin" for "thank-you", but decided not to try the pronounciation.

Tim gave her his prepared story that he was a prospector and had got lost on the waterways. She said, "You must be tired and hungry. Will you come up to my house for some food and a cup of tea?" He thanked her and they went to a small frame home and the first thing he noticed was a beautiful picture. It was Marion Young, dressed in her scarlet Royal Canadian Mounted Police uniform.

"This must be your daughter?" he offered.

"Yes, she is my only child and that is her graduation picture from the R.C.M.P. some years ago. She is visiting me for a week or so and right now she is out helping the men get ready for the trapping season. You didn't see her did you? I always worry about her but I know she is very good at living off the land in the bush."

He lied, "No I didn't see her." "Do you have a radio-telephone where we could call an airline base? I want to get a flight home as soon as possible."

"The closest place is a town named Longlac. There are some float planes stationed there. Would you like me to call them for you? By the way, my name is Julie Henry. Give me a few moments and I'll call them for you."

She returned and said, "This is your lucky day. A plane can be here in three hours. It is about one hundred and twenty miles one way so they should be able to pick you up here and then return back to their base by dark. Is that okay?"

He smiled, "that's wonderful and I thank you. It will be so great to get some clean clothes, a haircut, a bath and a shave. I do apologize for my looks. I would like to give you a gift. You can have my canoe and the camping equipment, I won't be needing them any longer. Do you mind if I wait in your house until the plane arrives?"

"You are certainly welcome. It's nice to have a new face to visit with. Oh! I'm sorry, I promised you lunch so give me a few moments," and Tim could hear the clanking of pots and the clinking of dishes.

They chatted about Indian conditions in their community and she was bitter about the lack of medical care and the increased use of alcohol in different communities because of unemployment. Tim didn't like the subjects discussed. He decided she might enter into a bitter dialogue about residential schools so before she had a chance he asked "do any of the Indian villages still have medicine men? I think they use to be called Shamans."

She smiled and said, "Yes, although most Indian communities don't admit to having any, there is generally one in each of the many communities."

"Do you think they really have a power of healing and telling the future?"

I don't know whether to believe them or not. There is a famous story about one Shaman who lived before the British or French discovered Canada. Would you like to hear about him?"

"Sure. Can you tell the story before the plane arrives?"

"okay, this fellow predicated the coming of the white man with his red flags. In Indian tradition and dialect, here is how it goes."

"Atsiluaq,

Angakunirataugajappuq,

HooooE HoooooE HoooooE HoooooE HoooooE

Kananilak, kingaaluni,

Saangania kanani,

Takujauppat,

Qallunaattaapik,

Aupaluttaapik,

Astiluarli,

Angakunirataugajappuq

HooooE HoooooE HoooooE HoooooE

"This is what it means in English. The Shaman sang this song predicting the arrival of the white man. The song later amazed everyone because the British and Hudson Bay Company both had red flags.

"I am going to try your language. Kinanaskomitin. I think it means thank-you."

Julie Henry replied, "it was nice meeting you. I'll tell my daughter about you. She will be sorry she didn't meet you. Good-bye and good luck."

The float plane headed in a southwards direction and Tim said, "Do you mind if we swing a little to the west, I'd like to see some of the waterways." Later he saw a canoe heading eastbound with a single paddler. He was escaping just in time. He figured he had a two day head start away from Marion Henry, the policewoman.

The pilot was paid and he directed Tim to a barbershop. He apologized for his appearance but the barber smiled and replied, "I've seen a lot of men come out of the bush and many look just like you."

He ordered the haircut, bought a shampoo and a shave then went to a men's wear store and bought two casual outfits including underwear, shoes and socks. At the motel, he soaped and soaked in the tub for over an hour. Then he stood a long time in the hot shower. He finally felt clean. At the local truck stop, he had a trucker's hot beef sandwich with coffee and after two refusals, a tractor-trailer driver agreed to take him to Toronto. His old clothes went into a garbage dumpster.

He opened his musty City apartment, lifted the windows for ventilation and put away some newly purchased groceries. After another hot shower, he made a phone call. It was to Ethel Grant in Texas.

CHAPTER 10

THE INVESTIGATION

The pre-programmed computers sent an over-due letter notice to any accounts that had not made their monthly payments after a thirty day waiting period. The letter was similar from all the financial institutions.

> *Dear Mr. Johnson,*
>
> *Our records indicate you have not made your monthly payment and it is now thirty days past-due. It is important that you remit this payment immediately. If you have made the payment, please disregard this letter. Thank you for your prompt attention to this notice.*
>
> *Yours Very Truly,*
> *Loan Manager*

About ten days later, the un-opened letters were returned and scrawled on the envelopes was written, "No such person at this address. Return to sender."

The Loan Officer hoped Mr. Johnson had moved with notification and he next tried the telephone. The automated reply said, "The telephone service at this number has been cancelled."

The Loan Manager reported these events to his Branch Manager who said, "Get in your car, drive over to Johnson's apartment, talk to the new tenant and the landlord. This doesn't sound good. I hope that bastard hasn't ripped us off."

The man answered the door and said, "Christ, are you another person looking for this guy Johnson. I don't know him and I don't know where he moved to. You might better talk to the landlord down the hall." The landlord said, "I know why you're here. Johnson moved about a month ago. I gave him his damage security deposit as I never saw an apartment so clean. Even the windows were sparkly clean He didn't leave me any forwarding address or telephone number. Give me your business card and if I hear anything about his whereabouts, I'll let you know. Sorry I couldn't be of more help."

Police Chief Roy Perrault couldn't believe the volume of phone calls from banks, credit card companies, co-op credit unions, mortgage companies and homeowners discovering they now had a first or second mortgage. Lawyers represented various embezzled people and companies and they were also calling the Chief. He said to himself, "My God, this looks like an epidemic." Over the intercom, he ordered his Chief Detective Peter Frederick to his office.

"Peter, we've got a white collar crime that looks pretty big. A bunch of financial places have been cheated, embezzled or tricked out of a lot of money. Everybody is phoning me and asking us to catch this fellow. I know you're busy with a bunch of other cases but I want you to transfer your files to some of the other detectives and work on this Johnson case. It looks like, on the surface, he might have got over a million dollars. Nobody knows where he's gone. Go and get whatever information you can from these people that claim they have been ripped off. If you need help, assign some detectives to help you. The media don't know about this embezzlement so keep it quiet for now."

Frederick called in Detectives Ray Eves who specialized in accounting, Doug Brown, trained in D.N.A. and junior Detective Jim Bell.

"Here are some of the jobs we need to do. Go over his apartment for fingerprints and search things such as hair in the drains and toilet for D.N.A.

evidence. Do the same with the rental car. The new tenant might not let you in so get a Judge's order if you need one.

All the banks have videos of this guy Johnson so I want copies made for our identification guys. We want samples of his signatures and I want interviews of any people that talked and had dealings with Johnson.

I want you to have interviews with his landlord, friends and girlfriends. Someone should have some information that might lead us to this guy. I want his telephone records checked, too.

I suspect he was from another city and was trained in banking systems and methods of embezzlement. We can assume he was wearing some type of disguise and he must have had help in the purchase of materials and using them. Also, somebody, like an engraver has made false papers; a driver's license, medical cards, social insurance and maybe a passport.

Lastly, I want the bank employee's records checked including the Loan Officer and the Branch Manager. I doubt if there was collusion but let's check it out. Also let's see if any of them are throwing around a lot of money like buying a new car, a boat, taking an expensive trip, acquiring a new girlfriend, going to casinos or buying a big home.

Oh yes, we can guess the name Larry Johnson was a pseudonym but on the chance it was his real name, I want to know if anybody by that name has disappeared for a year or so.

Sorry, another thing. This guy learned a lot about cheating financial places. We need to check with insurance companies and accounting companies to see if one of their knowledgeable senior employees left their company, took a leave of absence and can't account for their whereabouts

Report back in ten days and the Chief wants to be at our meeting. We all have a lot of work to do, so, good luck"

Peter Frederick phoned an old friend, Detective Mary Aylesworth in Toronto. He explained the crime. "Mary, this guy got away with between one and two million dollars. We're not sure exactly how much yet. Can you keep your eyes and ears open for someone with a lot of new money. Expensive car, hiring high priced prostitutes, wearing two thousand dollar suits or maybe hitting the race tracks with big bets. My Police Chief has dumped this whole thing on my lap and I can use all the help I can get. Maybe your foot patrols or under-cover guys might have noticed something new and unusual. I'd appreciate if you would let me know if somebody might fit the bill."

"Peter, you know I have nothing better to do than find your crooks for you. I'm kidding. I'll be of any help I can. Just remember, the next time you are in Toronto, you owe me a steak and lobster dinner."

His next call was to a Private Detective, Bill Lindsay. "There's a guy that was going by the name of Larry Johnson. Somebody, like an engraver, made a bunch of ID cards, driver's license, passport and medical. You know the really good ones in Toronto and I want you to see if you can find anything about this Johnson fellow."

"Peter, I'll be happy to look into it for you. My fee is one hundred dollars an hour plus expenses. I also might have to plunk down some bribery money. Do you want me to start?"

"Yea, we've got a lot of pressure on us to catch this guy. He ripped off a lot of financial places and they are hot on our tail to solve their bad loaning practices. Try and keep the costs under two thousand dollars. Thanks. We'll talk later."

The meeting was on Friday morning at eight a.m. complete with watery office coffee and Peter had bought a dozen donuts. Police Chief said to Peter, "I'll just listen to the reports and I'll add anything if it is beneficial to the meeting. So go ahead"

Peter started. "My contact in Toronto, Mary Aylesworth, detective, has done quite a bit of research. She has found some new high spenders who are betting the ponies, dating high-priced hookers, driving new sport cars and dressing to the nines. However, all of them have been under investigation and they are all getting rich with drug money and protection racketeering She is sure they had nothing to do with an embezzlement. Most of them will soon be arrested and we can compare DNA evidence at that time. That is, assuming we have anything for comparisons.

My guy, a P.I. named Bill Lindsay cannot get anyone to admit to a forgery for this Johnson guy. He thinks that maybe Johnson gave somebody really big bucks to keep their mouth shut and maybe threatened them physically if they squealed to anybody. Anyhow, it has been a dead-end try."

He continued, "The telephone records gave us nothing. Johnson called the local financial places many times, tee-off times at the golf club and ordered Chinese and pizza a few times. He made no calls out-of-town. There were no contacts that helped us."

Detective Ray Eves reported on the investigation of the bank employees and their managers. "I found nothing unusual. It was a big job so I had to borrow some accounting type investigators from other police forces. There was a group won ten thousand dollars on a government lottery but they split it six ways and it was all legit. One loan officer spent seven thousand dollars for his daughters wedding but he had to borrow part of it from the bank. Otherwise, everything seemed normal with everyone and we couldn't find a hint of collusion."

Detective Jim Bell reported on the sweep for fingerprints. "The tenant didn't want to let us in but we told him we would return with a Judge's Order so finally he co-operated. Johnson had cleaned the place with a heavy-duty solvent. The scene was contaminated with the new tenant but we found no old prints. We checked drain pipes and cracks in the floor but, they too, had been cleaned and vacuumed. Even the windows were sparkling bright. We think Johnson may have been wearing gloves in the apartment and maybe even booties over his shoes or slippers. The same thing goes for the rental car. The rental dealer said he had never had a car returned so clean. Again, the car has been rented several times since Johnson's disappearance and there are fingerprints all over the car from other people. The car dealer said the car was 'wickedly' clean."

Detective Bell continued. "We got several bank videos and the experts are sure he was wearing a disguise. Anyhow, an artist is making a picture of what he might look like without the disguise and we should have that soon. If this guy has no previous record, then he is tough to catch. If he has ever been arrested then we can compare partial prints, his looks without the disguise, the handwriting from a graphologist expert even if he did change hands, a possible iris scanner, a possible DNA comparison, a biometric eye and retina scanner, medical and dental records and even footprints. However, we have to get some evidence on Johnson first so we can do comparisons.

An interesting thing was discovered. Johnson signed a lot of papers for the various financial institutions. First we think he was right-handed and signing with his left. We also think he placed something like glue or polish on his fingers. There was no clear print on any of the many documents he signed but we think we got some partials. They could hold up in Court if we ever locate him for a comparison."

"One final thing," added the Chief Detective. "None of the insurance companies or crime labs know of anyone with Johnson's expertise that disappeared for over a year." He concluded to his Chief of Police, "We haven't got any evidence that will capture the ghostly Larry Johnson. So with your permission, we will keep the case open and hope he slips up somewhere."

Chief Perrault said, "Thanks for your excellent work and the quickness. I think we will catch Johnson but for now, let's get back to business as usual."

A bulletin was received several months later about the discovery of a bearded man from Rochester, New York State. It was signed by Marion Young of the Royal Canadian Mounted Police. A man had been at an isolated lake in Northern Ontario. No crime had been committed. He might have witnessed an airplane crash or had some information about a pilot, named Daniel Roche a.k.a. "Ace", who has been missing for several months and presumed dead in a sea-plane crash. He had flown from the northern village of Ogoki, Ontario to Longlac, Ontario. We have no further record of his whereabouts. The report was filed away by the various Police Groups across Canada.

CHAPTER 11

ETHEL GRANT

Her phone rang at home. "Ethel, you may not remember me. My name is Harry Bennett and about two years ago you taught me about disguises. Do you remember that?"

"Yes, certainly. It was very unusual. Did your disguise work? I've always wondered why you wanted it. You told me some cock and bull story about needing the disguise for an acting part but I didn't believe you. I figured you were going to rob a bank or something like that."

"Ethel, I need somebody to work for me in a very confidential way. I'm here in Texas. Can we get together? I can meet you almost any time. You set the time."

I'm still at the same old job. How about this coming Sunday?"

"Sure, that's great. Let's have dinner somewhere. You pick the place. Make it somewhere where we can have some privacy."

Ethel and Tim met at an exclusive and expensive restaurant. After all, it wasn't often she got invited out and even before she arrived, she had decided on steak and lobster.

Tim ordered the wine and he told the waiter not to hurry.

"Ethel, I need someone to carry out some errands for me. I might tell you I'm from Canada and I want someone helping me that the Police don't know. You won't be committing any crime but the Police will want to know who you are working for and my real identity. I might tell you now, my name is not Harry Bennett and I'll tell you my real name after you hear my story and agree to work for me. Can you get a couple of weeks off work and come to Canada? I have a two bedroom apartment. You can stay in one of the bedrooms and I'll promise you now, there will be nothing sexual happening. If you want, you can even bring a friend but she can't know anything about your work. All your expenses will be paid and you will receive one thousand a week for your time."

Ethel sipped her wine. *She thought, "don't get drunk. This sounds like serious business involving the Cops in a strange Country."*

"Okay. Whatever your name is. You talk and I'll listen. For now, I'll take it easy on the wine. Go ahead."

Tim started. "I'm an expert on white collar crime and in particular, something called embezzlement. I was offered a big payday by someone who wanted me to embezzle over a million dollars from a bunch of financial places, like banks, mortgage companies, credit card people and so on. I used your disguise and over a year or so ago, I managed to steal all this money. Then I disappeared from the community. I have all this money stored away in a safe place and intend to return it. In the meantime, I know the Police are looking for me. I also want to collect my pay from this fellow who hired me. I want someone like you to carry out some errands for me. You will be of great interest to the Police but you won't be doing anything illegal. However, they will try and find me through you. You will need a lot of skills to keep them from finding me. I'll stop now and let you ask any questions"

Ethel was quiet and said, "While we are eating dinner, let me think about it. You probably can guess, I have never been involved in any crimes before and this makes me a little nervous but also, it sounds exciting."

"What is Canada like. I've heard about tons of snow, Indians, igloos, the Mounted Police, good fishing and hunting."

Tim smiled. "Toronto is just like any American big city. Subways, heavy traffic, a few great restaurants, a busy airport and a few million people live there. Way up north, the Country is isolated and I guess that's what Americans read about."

Ethel was not educated but she had the street smarts. If your name isn't Harry Bennett, what do you want me to call you? It must seem strange to hear me call you by a false name."

"Just for now, call me Tim. If we work together, you'll have my full name and address."

"If you pay me a thousand a week, who will get the reward money? I imagine the banks and other financial places have offered a nice reward for the person who finds the embezzler."

"I'll guess there is some nice reward money. It could be quite a bit. If you work for me, we can talk about that later. However, you can never tell the Cops who I am or where I live. It's possible, when I return the money you can manage to claim the reward, but it's premature now to discuss that. When you arrive at Pearson Airport on an Air Canada flight, wear a red scarf so I'll spot you right away."

In Toronto, Tim gave Ethel her instructions. "Take the train from here to Montreal. Go to a pay phone and tell the Police Dispatcher you want to speak to the Chief Detective. Take a bunch of quarters with you for the pay phone so there is no trace. Tell the Detective you want to meet with him and tell him it is regarding a Mr. Larry Johnson who is wanted for embezzlements. This may be their first clue about me and they will want to know who you are and your address. Give them your real name but no address. Tell him Larry Johnson is prepared to return the money and when he does, can all criminal charges be cancelled?" He won't be able to give you an answer until he checks with his Police Chief, the Crown Attorney and the financial places. Tell him you will be back in touch with him in a week and you'll expect an answer. They will probably follow you back to Toronto. Get off the train at Oshawa which is about thirty miles east of Toronto. Watch for any faces getting on the train with you and then getting off with you at Oshawa. Get on a Go train to Toronto. Catch a taxi at the train station and keep watching for a familiar face. If you still think they are following you, the next part is up to you to slip the tail. Maybe go in a restaurant in the front door, through the kitchen and out the back door. Keep watching. Catch taxis, go to department stores, catch another taxi and do whatever you think is necessary. Be creative and don't let them follow you here. Absolutely. All the plans are lost if they find me."

"I'll give you a letter to give to the Head Detective. Here it is;

My name, as you know it is Larry Johnson, wanted for embezzling certain financial institutions. This person, Ethel Grant, delivering this letter has my permission to discuss certain matters with you. My inquiry is this:

If all monies are returned with a reasonable rate of interest, can criminal charges, fines and imprisonment be dismissed, withdrawn and waived? Ethel Grant will want an answer and will contact you a week from now.

Larry Johnson. (not signed)

Chief Detective rushed in to the office of Police Chief Roy Perrault. "Chief, guess what? We may have our first break on the Johnson embezzlement case. Some girl is coming in to see me on behalf of Johnson."

Ethel Grant delivered the letter to the Detective. He read it and said, "I'll try and get an answer for you by next week. Can I have your address or phone number if I need to talk to you before next week?"

"I won't give you any information. I'm just delivering a letter and I'm prohibited to say anything more. And, no, there is no address or telephone number you can have." Ethel left heading for the train station.

Detective Frederick was prepared. He had two junior detectives prepared to follow her and also called Toronto Detective Mary Ellsworth. "We've got a possible break in the Johnson case. A woman by the name of Ethel Grant has just left by train for Toronto and we would like a tail to see if she can lead us to Johnson's whereabouts." Detective Aylesworth got the description and had undercover police waiting at Union Station in Toronto.

Ethel watched faces on her train. Two men, sitting separately looked suspicious. She left the Via passenger train one stop before Toronto. Both of the men she was watching also got off. One pretended to read a paper and the other stood near a window at the depot seemingly waiting to meet an incoming passenger. She caught the first Go train from Oshawa to Toronto and both men were still with her. At Toronto, the two following men disappeared in the arriving crowd and she didn't notice two more men watching her. She reckoned someone would be following her. At the taxi stand, she told the driver to take her to a restaurant, any restaurant, providing it was a few miles away. When she got out, a cab pulled up a few yards behind her and two men followed her to the restaurant. She ordered coffee and left her coat at her table and headed for the Ladies washroom. It appeared she would be returning to her booth. Ethel walked through the kitchen to the amazement of the kitchen staff and continued out a back door into an alley. She climbed a fence, walked through a residential back-yard and then up a short street where she hailed another taxi. The driver was told that she would like to sightsee a bit of Toronto and she rode for fifteen minutes. No other cab followed. She caught a downtown bus and then walked three blocks to Tim McKay's apartment.

"That was fun. They followed me to Toronto and then two more followed me. I shook them at a restaurant. I'll bet their boss is pissed off."

Tim said, "Good work. The next thing is, I imagine they have had an expert remove my disguise and they have an artist giving them a good idea what I really look like. I want you to give me a new disguise so I can move around. Maybe make me look like an old man."

"Sure, I can do that pretty quick. You'll look about eighty years of age but you have to walk and talk like an elderly man. I'll have you practice in the apartment."

Detective Frederick was annoyed. "How in hell did she get away from two of our detectives and two Under-Covers in Toronto? Unknown to her, we got her photograph and fingerprints. I wonder if she was from Canada? She had quite a southern accent. Let's check airline records about women traveling alone, embarking somewhere in the southern states. I want her fingerprints and picture run through the computer systems."

Assistant Crown Attorney Ross Tranmer said, "Something strange is going on. Here we have a man who just got away with around a million dollars and now he wants to give it back with interest. The point is, why did he do it.? It cost him a lot of money to live here for over a year, pay rent, lease a car, join golf clubs, a service club and take important financial people out for dinners. He must be well aware of the consequences like jail, a fine, community service work, loss of credit ratings, bad press write-ups and having a stigma in the community. There is something here we are not understanding as he obviously doesn't need the money. If it was just a big game to him, then he has a hell of a lot of money or maybe, there was a backer. And what would a backer gain by Larry Johnson's success? Maybe it was a bet? Johnson was a really smart fellow. Well, maybe we'll figure something out later. We do know a few things. He is probably living in Toronto as that's where Ethel Grant went. We do know the artist's rendition after taking away the disguise. We do know that he wants out of the embezzlement he committed because he wants to give the money back and with interest. We also know that Johnson bought disguise material and probably someone taught him their applications.

Detective Doug Brown reported the next day. "There have been over four hundred women from the south in the last week that have traveled by themselves to Toronto. However, tracing them is next to impossible. They came from many different airports in the south and most have a southern drawl. Some gave a phony address about where they were staying in Canada, some are returning from a holiday, some are still here on business and some have returned to the States. There are a few prostitutes giving Toronto a try. Ethel Grant may have been one of the four hundred or she might have been here for a month, a year or longer. Her fingerprints and photo have been sent to the F.B.I. but they have no record of any criminal activity. She appears clean in the U.S.A."

The Assistant Crown said, "I'll take Johnson's offer to the Crown Attorney, the Chief, the Mayor and to all the cheated financial places. Let's see what they want to do."

Victor Tobiah received a message on his private telephone. "Tim McKay speaking. My Agent, Ethel Grant will be delivering a message to you on Tuesday next. The meeting to be at your office at one p.m.

CHAPTER 12

LETTERS & MEETINGS

"I'm writing three letters and would like you to have your friend mail them from New York City."

Ethel was now enjoying the subterfuge, smiled and replied, "Let me guess. The post mark from New York might throw the Police off your trail. And, no fingerprints, right?"

"Exactly. And I want the letters dispatched by special delivery and registered. This will add importance to them. About one week after they are received, I want you to visit three people."

LETTER TO: MR. VICTOR TOBIAH

My part of the contract is completed. As you and your contacts can or may have discovered, over a million dollars was embezzled from several financial institutions. My emissary will call at your place one week from the date of this letter and you will give her five hundred thousand dollars plus two hundred thousand dollars for my expenses minus $4,396 already paid to me.

My expenses are detailed with this letter and although they exceeded this amount, I will accept a loss as we had an agreement. You will note there are such items as apartment rental, car rental, insurance, furnishing the apartment, golf club membership, entertainment, food, disguise instructions and disguise materials, camping gear, airline tickets, service club membership, gasoline and clothing.

Therefore, please give Ethel Grant $695,604 dollars and she will be carrying a satchel used for carrying this money. An armed body-guard will be with her.

Signed—Mr. Tim McKay aka Larry Johnson

The next letter was to the Police Chief.

Chief Roy Perrault,

As you are aware, many months ago, over a million dollars was embezzled from several financial institutions and individuals. I understand your Chief Detective Peter Frederick was in charge of the investigation. My inquiry is this: if the money is returned to the financially injured parties with a reasonable rate of interest calculated on a pro rata basis from the date of their loss, can you give me your assurance that there will be no charges laid? This would include no incarceration, fines or community service.

I do not wish to imply anything about the ability of your staff but I believe it is impossible to apprehend this writer. If we cannot come to an agreement then the embezzled monies will anonymously be given to charities.

I realize you will consult with Crown Attorney Beverly Cousins or Assistant Crown Ross Tranmer about this proposal.

Part of our agreement is no publicity will be given to the news media from any parties involved

My Agent, Ethel Grant will call on you in a week's time to receive your reply. If your reply is in the affirmative, then I will expect a written agreement wherein all parties agree to the aforesaid above terms.

Larry Johnson (assumed name)

The third letter was written to all the financially injured parties.

TO VARIOUS FINANCIAL INSTITUTIONS AND CERTAIN MORTGAGE HOLDERS.

This writer embezzled funds from you, several months ago. I have written the Chief of Police and the Crown Attorney proposing an offer. These monies can all be returned to you with a reasonable rate of interest. The conditions are that, (a) there would be no publicity and (b) there would be no penalty given to this writer such as jail time, fine or community service work.

I believe the Chief or one of his Detectives will be contacting you very shortly to confirm your acceptance or non-acceptance of this offer.

If the offer is not accepted, then the embezzled money will be given to several charities. This letter is asking you to be prepared with an answer, probably in the next ten days.

Larry Johnson (assumed name)

All the letters were addressed, stamped and mailed to Ethel's friend in New York City. A $100 bill was enclosed for the friend's trouble and she was given instructions not to open any of the envelopes, just mail them at the Grand Central Station Post Office Depot.

Lawyer John Zyistral admitted an old man shuffling into his office. "Yes, Sir, what can I help you with to-day?"

The old fellow removed his old fashioned hat, wig, mustache, and over-sized coat. The lawyer stared in amazement, "Well, I'll be God damned. Tim McKay! Where the hell have you been? I heard you went overseas for a trip then no one heard anymore from you. I called you several times but your phone was disconnected, Are you going to a masquerade party or something? What's with the old man costume?

Geez, I tried calling you several times for golf games, parties and dinners. A bunch of guys went to Las Vegas but we couldn't reach you to join us. We've missed you, buddy."

Tim interrupted. "John, I've got a long story to tell you and I guess it's time I need a lawyer. Have you got an hour or so to spare?" The lawyer replied, "God, it's good to see you again, Tim. Listen, can you come in tomorrow afternoon? I'm booked solid to-day with clients but I'll clear my appointment book tomorrow after lunch Maybe we can have dinner afterwards."

Tim said, "great. It's good to see you again, John. I'm wearing the old man costume for a reason so I'll put it back on now and I'll be wearing it tomorrow."

His Lawyer laughed as he watched Tim dress with the wig, mustache, hat and big coat. "I wish I had my camera. I'll see you tomorrow."

Tim started out the door and said, "John, by the way, don't mention to any of our friends that you saw me. As I said, I'll explain everything tomorrow. You'll be amazed at my story." The old man shuffled out into the street and a passing policeman nodded politely.

At one-thirty in the afternoon the next day, the old man walked into Lawyer Zyistral's office. The receptionist waved him in, put on her coat, hung a little sign on the window saying, 'closed for the afternoon', locked the door and left. He and his Lawyer shook hands and Tim again removed the hot and sweaty disguise. The Lawyer poured two generous drinks of brandy in crystal glasses and said, "Okay, my friend, tell me what sort of trouble you've gotten yourself into."

Tim started with his meeting with Victor Tobiah, told about his entry into the respected community, explained the embezzlements, his efforts at leaving no clues, his trip to the bush, the death of Daniel Roche in the seaplane, the arrival of the Indian Policewoman Marion Young, his escape back to civilization and his letters to the various people having an interest in the crime. He spoke about Ethel Grant and said how invaluable she had been and added she would be doing some errands for him in the next ten days. He explained he was sure by now the Police had an artist's composite picture of him and that was the reason for the old man's look.

Three glasses of brandy later, it was five in the afternoon. John had asked him questions as Tim told his story. He frowned and scowled at times and laughed out loud at some of Tim's adventures.

Tim was exhausted and the Lawyer said, "Well, let me tell you some of the possible troubles you might have. Just off the top, you are guilty of fraud which could carry up to fourteen years in prison plus a five thousand dollar fine for each embezzlement. Next, falsification of books or documents which could carry five years, next fraudulently impersonating a person which you did when you got the mortgages and that could get you ten years, then, mail fraud can get you up to two years. There is up to five years for a false statements or representation concerning your crooked mortgage scheme and up to two years for willfully making false statements under The Bank Act.

Tim, do you want me to continue? In addition to jail time, there are also some pretty hefty fines. If we went to Court and pleaded guilty, an angry Judge could give you half a million in fines and ten to fifteen years in jail."

"Okay John. I know I could be in serious trouble. Pour me another drink. What else do you want to know?"

"Ah, I think that's enough for now Tim. I guess if I searched the Criminal Code I could find more but for now, put on your silly costume and let's have some dinner."

At the restaurant, the Lawyer said. "Have Ethel deliver the letters to the Chief, the Crown and the financially injured Companies. Have her report back to us and we will go from there. And, by the way, tell her to keep on giving them the slip because they are sure to follow her. My God, they would like to get their hands on you! Tell me again about tipping over in the canoe with a load of wood. And I can't imagine you building a shit house. Tim, you're a wonder and I must say, an amazing fellow."

Ethel made her trip to collect Tim's money from Victor Tobiah. Tim had hired a bouncer to escort her back to Toronto. She would be carrying a lot of cash. In Tobiah's office, he said, "I have considered the amount of money and decided to pay him a fee of three hundred thousand dollars plus the expenses of two hundred thousand less the amount already paid." Ethel stared at him. "I have been instructed to collect six hundred and ninety five thousand, six hundred and four dollars and you have reduced the bet by two hundred thousand?" He loftily replied, "the amount was excessive and it shouldn't have been that high. I'll give you a suitcase with the money and you can tell Mr. McKay that is the end of our dealings." She took the money and retorted, "Mr. McKay will not be happy about you reneging but I am only the messenger and I'll tell him what you've said."

Tobiah snorted, "Is he going to sue me for the difference? I don't think so. Just tell him the deal is finished."

Ethel and her escort returned to Toronto. Tim was furious. He said, "next week, I'll be seeing that son-of-a-bitch and he sure has a surprise coming." The money was placed in a safety deposit box as he didn't want a huge deposit raising any red flags with the bank.

Her next trip was to see the Chief of Police. She knew, after their conversation, it would be again a cat-and-mouse follow-me-if-you-can game with the Police desperate to find the whereabouts of Larry Johnson.

Before Ethel's arrival, the interested parties, Perrault, Frederick, Eves, Brown, Bell, Tranmer and Cousins had a meeting. The Mayor was not included as they didn't want politics coloring the discussion. Chief Perrault was chairman.

"You have all read the letter from this Johnson fellow. To reiterate, he wants to give the money back plus interest and not have any penalties. Detective Frederick, before we make any decisions, do you think we can catch this guy?"

All eyes were on Frederick. "Chief, we've had no success and I don't think any new clues are going to show up now. We do know some things about him but we don't know his real name or where he lives. We have one more chance. His Agent, emissary or whoever she is, will be seeing us within a week. Our only chance is to try and follow her to Johnson. If we can catch him, then we can throw everything in the law books at him. If we can't find him, then the Crown will have to propose a deal that he can accept."

Beverly Cousin, Crown Attorney said, "We can make him a proposal that he might accept. A ten thousand dollar fine, restitution of the money plus interest and one hundred hours of community service. The community service could be lecturing school children on methods of avoiding crime and telling them about possible jail time for breaking the law. Johnson would serve no time in prison and there would be no publicity. The Crown thinks we can get a Judge to agree to this sentencing."

Detective Eves added, "She gave us the slip last time, including avoiding the Toronto Detectives. We can try again but she obviously has instructions about losing her tail. With the New York City post mark, following her to a residence in Toronto may be futile as Johnson could be in New York City. Or, the post mark could be a trick. Anyway, if we can get the Toronto bunko squad to help us, we can try again to track him down."

The Chief said, "Okay, let's try one more time. If we don't succeed then . . . is everybody in agreement with the Crown's offer?"

Everyone nodded their assent.

Ethel and Lawyer Zyistsral made their plans to visit the Police Chief. Ethel carried a small suitcase.

The Detectives were ready to again follow Ethel. Two were at the train station and two at the bus station. The Toronto Police would be notified when Ethel returned to Toronto. They were hoping Johnson had not moved to New York City.

The meeting consisted of Crown Attorney Beverly Cousins, Police Chief Perrault, Detective Peter Frederick, Lawyer John Zyistral and Ethel Grant. Cousins started the meeting by acknowledging Larry Johnson's letter and stated simply, "we have not yet decided on our course of action. His embezzlement was a very serious crime. Our investigation is incomplete and we should know our position within a week. There is nothing more to discuss today."

Lawyer Zyistral replied, "if his offer is not accepted, then the charities will benefit. Please don't delay your decision beyond your offer of a week. We can meet you in Toronto, here in your office or we will accept an offer by registered letter. Whatever your offer, all parties must be agreeable to the terms. No exceptions." He gave everyone his business card.

The Chief said, "Thanks for coming here to the meeting and I guess we are adjourned."

The lawyer went to the train station for his trip to Toronto and oddly, Ethel Grant bought a ticket to Montreal. The under-cover cops expected her to go to Toronto so they hurriedly changed their destination. The waiting Toronto Police were notified she was traveling east instead of west and they were relieved of their surveillance duties.

Ethel easily noticed the two men, one dressed in a business suit and the other appeared as a college student. In Montreal, Ethel went into a hotel and sat in the coffee shop watching for familiar faces. They were there. She then walked down the street and spotted the same men she saw on the train.

In another restaurant, in the washroom, she opened her suitcase, put on a red wig, a bright blue coat, high heels and walked past the two detectives. She caught a taxi to the airport, caught a plane to Toronto, took taxis to several different locations and then, being satisfied no one was following her, went partially by subway and walked to Tim McKay's apartment.

When the Officials realized they had lost her again, a registered letter was sent to McKay's Lawyer. It read:

> *Mr. Zyistral,*
>
> *If Mr. Larry Johnson will turn himself into the Police, re-pay the stolen money plus interest and agree to a $10,000. fine (ten thousand dollars) and do one hundred hours of community social work within the next twelve months, then we will agree and give him a forgiveness release for the embezzlement crimes. The details of this offer can be completed if your client agrees in principal to this offer.*
>
> Signed—*Ross Tranmer, Assistant Crown Attorney.*

Tim McKay sighed a breath of relief. "We will accept. My God, I will be glad when this stupid thing I did is finished.". He, Ethel and his Lawyer made an appointment to see the Police Chief. Money was recovered from Swiss bank accounts, various safety deposit boxes and re-deposited. A certified cheque for the $10,000 fine was issued payable to the Crown, In the Right of the Province of Ontario. Tim's lawyer said he would arrange the community service hours with a School Board in Toronto. A cheque would be issued the next day re-paying all the money embezzled.

The adventure was almost finished. Before they left for Toronto, Peter Frederick said, "Sometime I would like to meet with you and hear how you arranged such an elaborate scheme. I still don't know why you did it. Was it an adventure, a dare from someone, a bet that you couldn't do it?" You took an awful chance of going to jail and ruining your reputation. Since you repaid all the money, you obviously didn't do it for money." Tim started walking away. "Sorry, but I can't give you any information. All I can tell you it was a hell of an experience. By the way, did you know it was Ethel Grant that persuaded me to turn myself in to the Police? Was there a reward from the banks and the other embezzled Companies?"

The Detective said, "Yes, and a sizeable reward with everyone putting up money. Probably around twenty-five thousand dollars. Do you think she is entitled to it?"

"Absolutely. I'll have my lawyer look into it for Ethel. She could sure use the money."

Tim told Ethel and his lawyer to go and have some lunch. He would meet them later as he had one more matter to attend to with Victor Tobiah.

"You told me about the honesty of the members of your Eastern Ontario Gambler's Syndicate. I presume you collected a huge bet after I succeeded in embezzling over a million dollars?"

Tobiah smiled and said, "Yes. I did pretty well. I suppose you are here because I reduced your payment by two hundred thousand dollars?" Is that right?"

Tim said, "You're Goddamned right. I'm pissed off. Now, where is the rest of my money? Ethel said you thought the amount was excessive. We made a deal, you cheating bastard."

Tocbiah said, "Yes I offered you too much. So, are you going to sue me?"

Tim said, "no, but I have a surprise for you," and he pulled a tape out of his pocket. "Every conversation we've had has been recorded. I have settled my crime with the Police but they would love to know your involvement in this embezzlement. You will go to jail for your participation, pay a fine and your friendly betting syndicate will avoid you forever. Plus, you have several business operations and the publicity will kill you. Do you want to hear the tape? It begins, 'I have an unusual business proposition for you.' You can have this tape because I have more in a safety deposit box. Do you want to pay the two hundred thousand you are trying to cheat from me or shall I send the tape to the Police?"

Tobiah smiled and said, "You are a smart son-of-a-bitch. Okay, wait here, the bank is a few doors from here and I'll get you the money."

Tim met Ethel and John at the restaurant and said, 'okay, let's go home, I'm satisfied" and Ethel knew what he meant.

That night, they had an expensive dinner. He gave her an envelope with $4,000 dollars. "Ethel, here is your pay. You did a great job and I admire your ability. If you want to stay for a while in Toronto, you are welcome to continue staying at my place." He told her that his Lawyer had a good possibility of getting her the reward money of $25,000 dollars. Ethel grinned with delight.

The candlelight complimented her ivory skin. She wore no jewelry and only a little blush plus eye make-up. At the apartment, he kept true to his word. He gave her a brotherly-type kiss goodnight and went to his bedroom. It was 2 a.m. and his door opened. She whispered, "Can I come in?" He watched as the silk black nightgown slipped to the floor. They kissed and he said, "That was beautiful."

The lovemaking started slowly. Her touch had a magical effect on him. As he explored her body, her sensations became alive. They moved in unison, force against force and then blended into oneness. In the morning, the lovemaking almost seemed perfect. They both slept with exhaustion.

At noon, they ate eggs benedict and drank coffee at the nearby hotel. Tim said, "Ethel, after you return to Texas, would you consider a marriage proposal? I know this place is not very romantic but your plane leaves soon and I had to ask you now."

Ethel looked in his eyes. "Tim, you are the best fellow I've ever met. I will call you from Texas to-night with my answer. At the airport they walked hand-in-hand and had a lover's kiss good-bye. That night, his phone rang. He picked it up, hope against hope and a woman's voice said softly, "yes".

CHAPTER 13

ALTRUISM

Tim had a guilty conscience. It had never been his nature to be dishonest but he could not deny he had been a thief, crook, liar, impersonator and dishonorable. His introspection was causing insomnia and mental agitation. There was the paradox wherein he had partially beaten the legal system but he had caused grief and upsetting circumstances to several surprised new mortgage holders and to Ace's family. He was contented without regret that he had outwitted the police considering all of their detection systems and anti-crime abilities.

He and Ethel had bought a four bedroom home with all the bells and whistles. Tim drove a Lexus and Ethel a Volkswagon convertible. Life was sweet.

The Press had not noticed his out-of-Court embezzlement settlement which left his lecturing business un-tarnished. It was returning $300,000 a year and he had received $500,000 tax free from Victor Tobiah. Lecturing at a University gave him a nice additional income and he occasionally appeared on radio and T.V. talk shows which he did for the promotional value of his business. Ethel was volunteering with costumes, back-drops and make-up for a non-profit local theatre.

They were becoming noticeable in the financially elite black-tie society and it amused Tim to think their magnificence would not be so gratuitous if they knew of his nefarious background.

Tim made a decision.

On a Sunday morning with his first coffee and morning newspaper he said to Ethel. "I bought an old edition of a newspaper from a small northern town and I want to read it to you. It said,

The search has been discontinued for floatplane pilot, Daniel Roche, better known as simply 'Ace'. His fellow pilots, friends and the Military Search and Rescue Unit have flown a huge grid but without success. It has now been several years since his disappearance but due to the immensity of the area and the thickness of the bush, there has been no discovery. A rumor persists that an unknown person may have been aboard with Ace but there was no entry in the log book and no witness has come forward about this mysterious person.

Tim added, "I got a copy of the obituary notice and it reads;

A service will be at Matthews United Church 1 p.m. Friday for Daniel Roche. He leaves his loving wife Blanche and two children, Amy and Jacque. Also, he is dearly remembered by his parents Cecille and Michael. Donations may be given to a charity of your choice. Rev. Reginald St. Laurent, B.A., D.D., will be officiating. Guests are invited to the Church Hall for refreshments after the Service.

"Ethel, I have to go back up north to the camp site. The family will never get closure until they discover the crash site and Ace's body."

She smiled and said, "Tim, I know it has been bothering you. I agree that you should do this for Ace's family. I think you should do it as quickly as possible. I know you will feel some relief."

At John Zyisgtral lawyer' office, Tim said, "John, I've got some instructions for you. I'm going back to my hide-out at the camp site. It was smart-ass flying but I feel obligated to give the family closure. I want you to hire me a pilot to take me to the camp site. I've purchased navigational equipment to pin-point the crash location. I want the Pilot to get full credit for locating the site and I don't want my name disclosed.

Secondly, I want to give his wife five thousand dollars in cash. Have a local lawyer handle the transaction and it will be by an anonymous friend. Thirdly, it is possible there could be a criminal offence when I didn't tell the authorities the whereabouts of a body. I don't want the Police involved and I guess my name can be kept secret under something called the Solicitor—Client Act.

Tim flew to his campsite and again marveled at the beauty of the land. At the site, the tent had fallen down and was a green blob of canvass laying at the water's edge. The table and backhouse were still in good useable shape. Tim said to the Pilot, "Give me a few minutes." He viewed the lake and remembered the drift wood, biting bugs, storms, the isolation and the wildlife. Finally the Pilot said, "Let's go." Tim aimed the directional equipment at the crash site and showed the Pilot distance and direction. Soon, buried deep in a thick black forest, a tiny bit of the wing could be seen.

The location was given to the Police and the family. The Pilot would say he had seen it, quite by accident. Tim returned home.

He told Ethel, "I need your help with my next project. There were several families that were devastated when they found a first or second mortgage on their homes. They were likely bewildered, worried and visibly shaken." He asked Ethel to personally deliver an envelope containing one thousand dollars to each family. He added, "Make sure the owners get the money and if they ask you about the reason, deny any knowledge and tell them you are just a paid messenger. There is a letter inside the envelope. It says;

A few years ago, you discovered you had a mortgage on your home. I know this caused you a great amount of worry and consternation. Most of you worked hard to buy your home and I regret causing you this problem. I know the situation has been resolved but I would like to give you small gift of $1,000 for your troubles.

I know most of you, in the vernacular would 'wring my neck' or in the least, show your anger towards me. I realize the financial matter has been resolved but I would like to give you this small gift of $1000 which is my way of apologizing.

The messenger is not aware of the contents so she cannot give you any explanation or information.

I hope this money will give you some enjoyment.

Unsigned

Ethel returned home after two days and said, "Most of them didn't know whether to laugh or cry. They all wanted to know who you are. I think most of them would like to vent their rage towards you but I just simply denied any knowledge."

His last item for the culmination of the embezzlement was obeying the Judge's order for one hundred hours of community service and he knew exactly how to achieve this Order.

The acquiescence of the Church Elders, the Minister and the Officer handling Community Service sentencing agreed to a new youth group. The Presbyterian Church gratuitously donated the use of their Church basement on Sunday nights from seven until nine. An announcement was made at several Churches and at the first meeting, six teenagers attended.

Tim explained his plans. "This is not a religious group and I guess you will eventually find a name for it. We will have some guest speakers from time to time. On the religious side, we might have a Protestant Minister, a Catholic Priest, a Rabbi, a Hindu spokesman and yes, even Atheism. But, these speakers will be just a small part of our activities. Tonight, we have a small group so next week, invite a friend and I'll tell you more about my plans and thoughts. Maybe, to-night, we could just play some games.

The following week there were fifteen teens. Tim explained, "This group is going to have a good time. Last week, I mentioned possible speakers. We can have dances, trips, games in the summer and spring such as softball and soccer. We can have discussion groups on any subject you want. I have solicited some of the big companies in the Toronto area. We are getting a billiard table, an indoor shuffleboard court, a ping-pong table and a bocce game. Some Sunday nights we could go bowling or visit a major league ball game. I think it would be nice to visit nursing homes and senior citizen residences.

There are just a few rules for attendance. Firstly, you must be over the age of thirteen and under nineteen. If anyone, anyone at all, arrives here with the smell of beer or liquor on their breath, they will be asked to leave and they will never, never, be permitted here again. If I discover you are on soft or hard drugs, again, you will be asked to leave. You will not return.

You should have a President, a vice-President and a Secretary Treasurer. Next week we will have an election. We will also collect fifty cents per meeting. That will cover certain expenses you will have like food and drinks after a meeting.

Tonight, I want you to tell me what subjects or topics you would like discussed." Hands started flying up and Tim made a note of their ideas. He later read them back. "Here are some of your topics we might have; capital punishment, homosexuality, mixed marriages, abortion, addiction to cigarettes, booze and drugs, cruelty to animals, life in prison, legal protection for the poor and homeless street people."

Tim added, "Some things you might consider are fund raising projects for worthwhile charities, pot luck dinners, competition games night and inter-Club meetings with other Clubs with the same values."

The following week there were sixty teens and in the sixth month, over a hundred were in attendance. On three occasions, Tim made a person leave because of the smell of beer. They pleaded to return but were firmly denied.

He had not expected romances to flourish. Once he caught two fourteen year old teens starting to undress each other in a closet. Several were holding hands during the meetings and a little kissing was done on the sly. Finally, Tim asked that their romances not be pursued at the meetings. He hoped against hope that no girl would get pregnant during her membership. Luckily, it didn't happen.

He was pleased that most of them had confidence in him and that he wasn't unduly harsh with his rules. He was pleased when some would ask for his advice, usually some problem at home.

Tim could not believe his teen association had now passed two hundred hours. He submitted his resignation to the Community Service Provincial representative who, in turn, notified the original sentencing Judge. He received a lovely scroll and a letter of congratulations from the Court and a sincere thank-you-note from the Clerk of Session at the Church. Even the Mayor of the City awarded him a plaque and he had a small write-up in the newspaper.

It was time to concentrate on his marriage. That night, Ethel cooked lobster, baked pepper squash and warm cheese rolls. She said, "You know you have a birthday soon and I've been thinking of a present for you." Tim replied, "I think I would like to go back to the northern camp-site, with you of course, and relive some of those escape days. Would you be interested?"

With the glow of wine, she answered, "Tim, I've already bought your present. It is a two week luxury cruise leaving from Miami. I am not going to suffer from insect bites, storms, mysterious animals, outdoor toilets, lack of wood, dried food and God knows what other discomforts but our holiday will start when we hear the Captain announce. ALL ABOARD."

Tim smiled at the double entendre. With the flickering candles over their dinner table, the embezzler felt grateful for having this soul mate who had enhanced and added a quiet beauty and wisdom to his life.